ALDOUS HUXLEY (1894-1963)

A member of a family which distinguished itself in many fields of intellectual endeavor, Aldous Huxley was most famous as a man of letters. A critic, a poet and an essayist, he wrote with wit and authority on architecture, science, music, philosophy, history and religion. It was, however, in his novels that he made his most deeply-felt statements about the nature of man and the world in which he lived.

APE AND ESSENCE is Huxley's most chilling allegory, a terrifying prophecy set in southern California in 2108.

APE AND ESSENCE

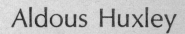

Aldous Huxley

A PERENNIAL CLASSIC
Harper & Row, Publishers
New York

APE AND ESSENCE

Copyright © 1948 by Aldous Huxley

First PERENNIAL CLASSIC edition published 1972

STANDARD BOOK NUMBER: 06–083100–6

3-74

Ape and Essence

TALLIS

IT WAS the day of Gandhi's assassination; but on Calvary the sightseers were more interested in the contents of their picnic baskets than in the possible significance of the, after all, rather commonplace event they had turned out to witness. In spite of all the astronomers can say, Ptolemy was perfectly right: the center of the universe is here, not there. Gandhi might be dead; but across the desk in his office, across the lunch table in the Studio Commissary, Bob Briggs was concerned to talk only about himself.

"You've always been such a help," Bob assured me, as he made ready, not without relish, to tell the latest installment of his history.

But at bottom, as I knew very well and as Bob himself knew even better than I, he didn't really want to be helped. He liked being in a mess and, still more, he liked talking about his predicament. The mess and its verbal dramatization made it possible for him to see himself as all the Romantic Poets rolled into one—Beddoes committing suicide, Byron committing fornication, Keats dying of Fanny Brawne, Harriet dying of Shelley. And seeing himself as all the Romantic Poets, he could forget for a little the two prime sources of his misery—the fact that he had none of their talents and very little of their sexual potency.

"We got to the point," he said (so tragically that it occurred to me that he would have done better as an actor than as a writer of screen plays), "we got to the point, Elaine and I, where we felt like . . . like Martin Luther."

"Martin Luther?" I repeated in some astonishment.

"You know—*ich kann nicht anders*. We just couldn't —but *couldn't*—do anything but go off together to Acapulco."

And Gandhi, I reflected, just couldn't do anything but resist oppression nonviolently and go to prison and finally get shot.

"So there it was," he went on. "We got on a plane and flew to Acapulco."

"Finally!"

"What do you mean, *'finally'*?"

"Well, you'd been thinking about it for a long time, hadn't you?"

Bob looked annoyed. But I remembered all the previous occasions when he had talked to me about the problem. Should he or should he not make Elaine his mistress? (That was his wonderfully old-world way of putting it.) Should he or should he not ask Miriam for a divorce?

A divorce from the woman who in a very real sense was still what she had always been—his only love; but in another very real sense Elaine was also his only love—and would be still more so if he finally decided (and that was why he couldn't decide) to "make her his mistress." To be or not to be—the soliloquy had gone on for the best part of two years, and if Bob could have had his way it would have gone on for ten years longer. He liked his messes to be

2

chronic and mainly verbal, never so acutely carnal as to put his uncertain virility to yet another humiliating test. But under the influence of his eloquence, of that baroque façade of a profile and prematurely snowy hair, Elaine had evidently grown tired of a merely chronic and platonic mess. Bob was presented with an ultimatum: it was to be either Acapulco or a clean breach.

So there he was, bound and committed to adultery no less irrevocably than Gandhi had been bound and committed to nonviolence and prison and assassination, but, one may suspect, with more and deeper misgivings. Misgivings which the event had wholly justified. For, though poor Bob didn't actually tell me what had happened at Acapulco, the fact that Elaine was now, as he put it, "acting strangely" and had been seen several times in the company of that unspeakable Moldavian baron, whose name I have fortunately forgotten, seemed to tell the whole ludicrous and pathetic story. And meanwhile Miriam had not only refused to give him a divorce: she had taken the opportunity of Bob's absence and her possession of his power of attorney to have the title to the ranch, the two cars, the four apartment houses, the corner lots at Palm Springs and all the securities transferred from his name to hers. And meanwhile he owed thirty-three thousand dollars to the Government for arrears of income tax. But when he asked his producer for that extra two hundred and fifty dollars a week which had been as good as promised him, there was only a long and pregnant silence.

"What about it, Lou?"

Measuring his words with a solemn emphasis, Lou Lublin gave his answer.

3

"Bob," he said, "in this Studio, at this time, not even Jesus Christ himself could get a raise."

The tone was friendly; but when Bob tried to insist, Lou had banged his desk and told him that he was being un-American. That finished it.

Bob talked on. But what a subject, I was thinking, for a great religious painting! Christ before Lublin, begging for a raise of only two hundred and fifty bucks a week and being turned down flat. It would be one of Rembrandt's favorite themes, drawn, etched, painted a score of times. Jesus turning sadly away into the darkness of unpaid income tax, while in the golden spotlight, glittering with gems and metallic highlights, Lou in an enormous turban still chuckled triumphantly over what he had done to the Man of Sorrows.

And then there would be Breughel's version of the subject. A great synoptic view of the entire Studio; a three-million-dollar musical in full production, with every technical detail faithfully reproduced; two or three thousand figures, all perfectly characterized; and in the bottom right-hand corner long search would finally reveal a Lublin, no bigger than a grasshopper, heaping contumely upon an even tinier Jesus.

"But I've had an absolutely stunning idea for an original," Bob was saying with that optimistic enthusiasm which is the desperate man's alternative to suicide. "My agent's absolutely crazy about it—thinks I ought to be able to sell it for fifty or sixty thousand."

He started to tell the story.

Still thinking of Christ before Lublin, I visualized the scene as Piero would have painted it—the composition, luminously explicit, an equation in balanced voids and solids, in harmonizing and contrasting hues; the figures in adamantine repose. Lou and his assistant

4

producers would all be wearing those Pharaonic head-dresses, those huge inverted cones of white or colored felt, which in Piero's world serve the double purpose of emphasizing the solid-geometrical nature of the human body and the outlandishness of Orientals. For all their silken softness, the folds of every garment would have the inevitability and definitiveness of syllogisms carved in porphyry and throughout the whole we should feel the all-pervading presence of Plato's God, forever mathematizing chaos into the order and beauty of art.

But from the Parthenon and the *Timaeus* a specious logic leads to the tyranny which, in the *Republic*, is held up as the ideal form of government. In the field of politics the equivalent of a theorem is a perfectly disciplined army; of a sonnet or picture, a police state under a dictatorship. The Marxist calls himself scientific and to this claim the Fascist adds another: he is the poet—the scientific poet—of a new mythology. Both are justified in their pretensions; for each applies to human situations the procedures which have proved effective in the laboratory and the ivory tower. They simplify, they abstract, they eliminate all that, for their purposes, is irrelevant and ignore whatever they choose to regard as inessential; they impose a style, they compel the facts to verify a favorite hypothesis, they consign to the waste paper basket all that, to their mind, falls short of perfection. And because they thus act like good artists, sound thinkers and tried experimenters, the prisons are full, political heretics are worked to death as slaves, the rights and preferences of mere individuals are ignored, the Gandhis are murdered and from morning till night a million school-teachers and broadcasters proclaim the infallibility of the bosses who happen at the moment to be in power.

5

"And after all," Bob was saying, "there's no reason why a movie shouldn't be a work of art. It's this damned commercialism . . ."

He spoke with all the righteous indignation of an ungifted artist denouncing the scapegoat whom he has chosen to take the blame for the lamentable consequences of his own lack of talent.

"Do you think Gandhi was interested in art?" I asked.

"Gandhi? No, of course not."

"I think you're right," I agreed. "Neither in art nor in science. And that's why we killed him."

"We?"

"Yes, we. The intelligent, the active, the forward-looking, the believers in Order and Perfection. Whereas Gandhi was a reactionary who believed only in people. Squalid little individuals governing themselves, village by village, and worshiping the Brahman who is also Atman. It was intolerable. No wonder we bumped him off."

But even as I spoke I was thinking that that wasn't the whole story. The whole story included an inconsistency, almost a betrayal. This man who believed only in people had got himself involved in the sub-human mass-madness of nationalism, in the would-be super-human, but actually diabolic, institutions of the nation-state. He got himself involved in these things, imagining that he could mitigate the madness and convert what was satanic in the state to something like humanity. But nationalism and the politics of power had proved too much for him. It is not at the center, not from within the organization, that the saint can cure our regimented insanity; it is only from without, at the periphery. If he makes himself a part of the machine, in which the collective madness is incarnated, one or the other of two things is bound to happen. Either he remains himself, in which case the machine will use him as long as it can and, when he becomes unusable, reject or destroy him. Or he will be transformed into the likeness of the mechanism with and against which he works, and in this case we shall see Holy Inquisitions and alliances with any tyrant prepared to guarantee ecclesiastical privileges.

"Well, to get back to their disgusting commercialism," Bob said at last. "Let me give you an example . . ."

But I was thinking that the dream of Order begets tyranny, the dream of Beauty, monsters and violence. Athena, the patroness of the arts, is also the goddess of scientific warfare, the heavenly Chief of every General Staff. We killed him because, after having briefly (and fatally) played the political game, he refused any longer to go on dreaming our dream of a national Order, a social and economic Beauty; because he tried to bring us back to the concrete and cosmic facts of real people and the inner Light.

The headlines I had seen that morning were parables; the event they recorded, an allegory and a prophecy. In that symbolic act, we who so longed for peace had rejected the only possible means to peace and had issued a warning to all who, in the future, might advocate any courses but those which lead inevitably to war.

"Well, if you've finished your coffee," said Bob, "let's go."

We rose and walked out into the sunshine. Bob took my arm and squeezed it.

"You've been enormously helpful," he assured me again.

"I wish I could believe it, Bob."

"But it's true, it's true."

And perhaps it was true, in the sense that stirring the mess before a sympathetic public made him feel better, more like the Romantics.

We walked on for a little in silence—past the Projection Rooms and between the Churrigueresque bungalows of the executives. Over the entrance to the largest of them a great bronze plaque bore the inscription, LOU LUBLIN PRODUCTIONS.

"What about that salary raise?" I asked. "Shall we go in and have another shot at it?"

Bob uttered a rueful little laugh, and there was another silence. When at last he spoke, it was in a pensive tone.

"Too bad about old Gandhi," he said. "I suppose his great secret was not wanting anything for himself."

"Yes, I suppose that was one of the secrets."

"I wish to God I didn't want things so much."

"Same here," I fervently concurred.

"And when you finally get what you want, it's never what you thought it was going to be."

Bob sighed and relapsed into silence. He was thinking, no doubt, of Acapulco, of the horrible necessity of passing from the chronic to the acute, from the vaguely verbal to the all too definitely and concretely carnal.

We emerged from the street of executive bungalows, crossed a parking lot and entered a canyon between towering sound stages. A tractor passed, pulling a low trailer, on which was the bottom half of the west door of a thirteenth-century Italian cathedral.

"That's for 'Catherine of Siena.'"

"What's that?"

"Hedda Boddy's new picture. I worked on the script two years ago. Then they gave it to Streicher. And after that it was rewritten by the O'Toole-Menendez-Boguslavsky team. It's lousy."

Another trailer rattled past with the upper half of the cathedral door and a pulpit by Niccolò Pisano.

"When you come to think of it," I said, "she's very like Gandhi in some ways."

"Who? Hedda?"

"No, Catherine."

"Oh, I see. I thought you were talking about the loincloth."

"I was talking about saints in politics," I said. "They didn't actually lynch her, of course; but that was only because she died too young. The consequences of her politics hadn't had time to show up. Do you go into all that in the script?"

Bob shook his head.

"Too depressing," he said. "The public likes its stars to be successful. Besides, how can you talk about church politics? It would certainly be anti-Catholic and might easily become un-American. No, we play safe—concentrate on the boy she dictated her letters to. He's wildly in love—but it's all sublimated and spiritual, and after she's dead he goes into a hermitage and prays in front of her picture. And then there's the other boy who actually made passes at her. It's mentioned in her letters. We play that for all its worth. They're still hoping to be able to sign up Humphrey . . ."

A loud hooting made us both jump.

"Look out!"

Bob caught my arm and pulled me back. From the

courtyard in the rear of the Story Department a two-ton truck emerged into the roadway.

"Why don't you look where you're going?" shouted the driver as he passed.

"Idiot!" Bob yelled back; then, turning to me, "Do you see what it's loaded with?" he asked. "Scripts." He shook his head. "Taking them to the incinerator. Which is where they belong. A million dollars worth of literature."

He laughed with melodramatic bitterness.

Twenty yards up the road, the truck swung sharply to the right. Its speed must have been excessive; centrifugally propelled, half a dozen of the topmost scripts spilled out into the road. Like prisoners of the Inquisition, I thought, making a miraculous escape on the way to the stake.

"The man can't drive," Bob was grumbling. "One of these days he'll kill somebody."

"But meanwhile let's see who's been saved."

I picked up the nearest of the scripts.

"'A Miss is as good as a Male, Screenplay by Albertine Krebs.'"

Bob remembered it. It stank.

"Well, what about 'Amanda'?" I turned over the pages. "It must have been a musical. Here's some poetry.

"'Amelia needs a meal,
But Amanda needs a man . . .'"

Bob wouldn't let me go on.

"Don't, don't! It made four and a half million during the Battle of the Bulge."

I dropped "Amanda" and picked up another of the spread-eagled volumes. This one, I noticed, was bound in green, not in the Studio's standard crimson.

"'Ape and Essence,'" I read aloud from the hand-lettered front cover.

"'Ape and Essence'?" Bob repeated in some surprise.

I turned to the flyleaf.

"'An original Treatment by William Tallis, Cottonwood Ranch, Murcia, California.' And here's a note in pencil. 'Rejection slip sent 11-26-47. No self addressed envelope. For the Incinerator'—twice underlined."

"They get thousands of these things," Bob explained.

Meanwhile I was looking into the body of the script. "More poetry."

"Christ!" said Bob in a tone of disgust.

"'Surely it's obvious,'" I began reading:

"'Surely it's obvious.

Doesn't every schoolboy know it?

Ends are ape-chosen; only the means are man's.

Papio's procurer, bursar to baboons,

Reason comes running, eager to ratify;

Comes, a catch-fart with Philosophy, truckling to tyrants;

Comes, a pimp for Prussia, with Hegel's Patent History;

Comes with Medicine to administer the Ape-King's aphrodisiac;

Comes, rhyming and with Rhetoric, to write his orations;

Comes with the Calculate to aim his rockets

Accurately at the orphanage across the ocean;

Comes, having aimed, with incense to impetrate

Our Lady devoutly for a direct hit.'"

There was a silence. We looked at one another questioningly.

"What do you think of it?" Bob said at last.

I shrugged my shoulders. I really didn't know.

"Anyhow, don't throw it away," he went on. "I want to see what the rest is like."

We resumed our walk, turned a final corner and there, a Franciscan convent among palm trees, was the Writers' Building.

"Tallis," Bob was saying to himself, as we entered, "William Tallis . . ." He shook his head. "Never heard of him. And anyhow, where's Murcia?"

The following Sunday we knew the answer—knew it not merely in theory and on the map, but experimentally, by going there, at eighty miles an hour, in Bob's (or rather Miriam's) Buick convertible. Murcia, California, was two red gasoline pumps and a very small grocery store on the southwestern fringe of the Mojave desert.

The long drouth had broken two days before. The sky was still overcast and a cold wind blew steadily from the west. Ghostly under their roof of slate-colored cloud, the San Gabriel mountains were white with newly fallen snow. But to the north, far out in the desert, the sun was shining in a long narrow strip of golden light. All around us were the soft rich grays and silvers, the pale golds and russets of the desert vegetation—sagebrush, burrobrush, bunch grass and buckwheat, with here and there a strangely gesticulating Joshua tree, rough barked, or furred with dry prickles, and tufted at the end of its many-elbowed arms with thick clusters of green metallic spikes.

An old deaf man, at whom we had to shout our questions, at last understood what we were talking about. Cottonwood Ranch—of course he knew it. Take that dirt road there; drive south for a mile; then turn east, follow the irrigation ditch for another three quarters of a mile, and there it was. The old man wanted to tell us much more about the place; but Bob was too impatient to listen. He threw the car into gear and we were off.

Along the irrigation ditch the cottonwoods and willows were aliens, clinging precariously, in the midst of those tough ascetic lives of the desert, to another, easier, more voluptuous mode of being. They were leafless now, the mere skeletons of trees, white against the sky; but one could imagine how intense, under the fierce clear sun, would be the emerald of their young leaves three months from now.

The car, which was being driven much too fast, crashed heavily into an unexpected dip. Bob swore.

"Why any man in his senses should choose to live at the end of a road like this, I can't imagine."

"Perhaps he takes it a little more slowly," I ventured to suggest.

Bob did not deign so much as to glance at me. The car rattled on at undiminished speed. I tried to concentrate on the view.

Out there, on the floor of the desert, there had been a noiseless, but almost explosive transformation. The clouds had shifted and the sun was now shining on the nearest of those abrupt and jagged buttes, which rose so inexplicably, like islands, out of the enormous plain. A moment before they had been black and dead. Now suddenly they had come to life between a shadowed foreground and a background of cloudy darkness. They shone as if with their own incandescence.

I touched Bob's arm and pointed.

"Now do you understand why Tallis chooses to live at the end of this road?"

He took a quick look, swerved round a fallen Joshua tree, looked again for a fraction of a second and brought his eyes back to the road.

"It reminds me of that etching by Goya—you know the one. The woman riding a stallion, and the animal's turning its head and has her dress between its teeth—trying to pull her down, trying to tear the clothes off her. And she's laughing like a maniac, in a frenzy of pleasure. And in the background there's a plain, with buttes sticking out of it, just like here. Only if you look carefully at Goya's buttes, you see that they're really crouching animals, half rats, half lizards—as big as mountains. I bought a reproduction of it for Elaine."

But Elaine, I reflected in the ensuing silence, hadn't taken the hint. She had allowed the stallion to drag her to the ground; she had lain there, laughing and laughing, uncontrollably, while the big teeth ripped at her bodice, tore the skirt to shreds, grazing the soft skin beneath with a fearful but delicious threat, with the tingling imminence of pain. And then, at Acapulco, those huge rat-lizards had stirred out of their stony sleep, and suddenly poor old Bob had found himself surrounded, not by deliciously swooning Graces, not by the laughing troop of rosy-bottomed Cupids, but by monsters.

But meanwhile we had reached our destination. Between the trees along the ditch I saw a white frame house under an enormous cottonwood, with a windmill to one side of it, a corrugated iron barn to the other. The gate was closed. Bob stopped the car and we got out. A white board had been nailed to the gatepost. On it an unskilled hand had painted a long inscription in vermilion.

The leech's kiss, the squid's embrace,
　The prurient ape's defiling touch:
And do you like the human race?
　No, not much.

THIS MEANS YOU, KEEP OUT.

"Well, we've evidently come to the right place,"
I said.

Bob nodded. We opened the gate, walked across
a wide expanse of beaten earth and knocked at the
door of the house. It was opened almost immediately
by a stout elderly woman in spectacles, wearing a
flowered blue cotton dress and a very old red jacket.
She gave us a friendly smile.

"Car broken down?" she inquired.

We shook our heads and Bob explained that we
had come to see Mr. Tallis.

"Mr. Tallis?"

The smile faded from her face; she looked grave
and shook her head. "Didn't you know?" she said.
"Mr. Tallis passed on six weeks ago."

"Do you mean, he's dead?"

"Passed on," she insisted, then launched out into
her story.

Mr. Tallis had rented the house for a year. She
and her husband went to live in the little old cabin
behind the barn. It only had an outside toilet but
they had been used to that back in North Dakota,
and luckily it had been a warm winter. Anyhow they
were glad of the money, what with prices the way
they were nowadays; and Mr. Tallis couldn't have
been pleasanter, once you understood that he liked
his privacy.

15

"I suppose it was he who put up that sign on the gate?"

The old lady nodded and said that it was kind of cute; she meant to leave it there.

"Had he been sick for a long time?" I asked.

"Not sick at all," she answered. "Though he always did say he had heart trouble."

And that was why he had passed on. In the bathroom. She found him there one morning, when she came to bring him his quart of milk and a dozen eggs from the store. Stone cold. He must have laid there all night. She had never had such a shock in all her life. And then what a commotion on account of there not being any relatives that anybody knew about! The doctor was called and then the sheriff, and there had to be a court order before the poor man could even be buried, much less embalmed. And then all the books and papers and clothes had to be packed up and seals put on the boxes, and everything stored somewhere in Los Angeles, just in case there should be an heir somewhere. Well, now she and her husband were back in the house, and she felt rather badly about it, because poor Mr. Tallis still had four months of his lease to run and he'd paid everything in advance. But of course in one way she was thankful, now that the rain and snow had come at last—on account of the toilet being inside the house, not outside, like when they were living in the cabin.

She paused for breath. Bob and I exchanged glances.

"Well, in the circumstances," I said, "I think we'd better be going."

But the old lady wouldn't hear of it.

"Come in," she insisted, "come in."

We hesitated; then, accepting her invitation, followed her through a tiny entrance lobby into the living room. An oil stove was burning in a corner of the room; the air was hot and an almost tangible smell of fried food and diapers filled the house. A little old man like a leprechaun was seated in a rocking chair near the window, reading the Sunday comics. Near him a pale, preoccupied-looking young girl—she couldn't have been more than seventeen—was holding a baby in one arm and, with the other hand, buttoning her pink blouse. The child belched; a bubble of milk appeared at the corner of its mouth. The young mother left the final button undone and tenderly wiped the pouting lips. Through the open door of another room came the sound of a fresh soprano voice singing, "Now is the Hour," to the accompaniment of a guitar.

"This is my husband," said the old lady. "Mr. Coulton."

"Pleased to meet you," said the leprechaun, without looking up from his comics.

"And this is our granddaughter, Katie. She got married last year."

"So I see," said Bob. He bowed to the girl and gave her one of those fascinating smiles, for which he was so famous.

Katie looked at him as though he were merely a piece of furniture; then, fastening that final button, she turned without a word and started to climb the steep stairs that led to the upper floor.

"And these," Mrs. Coulton went on, indicating Bob and myself, "are two friends of Mr. Tallis."

We had to explain that we weren't precisely friends. All we knew of Mr. Tallis was his work; but that had interested us so much that we had come here, hoping to make his acquaintance—only to learn the tragic news of his death.

Mr. Coulton looked up from his paper.

"Sixty-six," he said. "That's all *he* was. I'm seventy-two myself. Seventy-two last October."

He uttered the triumphant little laugh of one who has scored a victory, then returned to Flash Gordon —Flash the invulnerable, Flash the immortal, Flash the perpetual knight errant to girls, not as they lamentably are, but as the idealists of the brassiere industry proclaim that they ought to be.

"I happened to see what Mr. Tallis had sent in to our Studio," said Bob.

Again the leprechaun looked up.

"You're in the movies?" he inquired.

Bob admitted that he was.

In the next room the music broke off suddenly in the middle of a phrase.

"One of those big shots?" Mr. Coulton inquired.

With the most charming false modesty, Bob assured him that he was only a writer who occasionally dabbled in directing.

The leprechaun nodded slowly.

"I see in the paper where that guy Goldwyn says all the big shots got to take a fifty per cent cut in their salary."

His eyes twinkled gleefully, once again he uttered his triumphant little laugh. Then abruptly disinteresting himself from reality, he returned to his myths.

Christ before Lublin! I tried to change the painful subject by asking Mrs. Coulton whether she had known that Tallis was interested in the movies. But as I spoke a sound of footsteps in the inner room distracted her attention.

I turned my head. In the doorway, dressed in a black sweater and a tartan skirt there stood—who? Lady Hamilton at sixteen, Ninon de Lenclos when she lost her virginity to Coligny, *la petite* Morphil, Anna Karenina in the schoolroom.

"This is Rosie," said Mrs. Coulton proudly, "our other granddaughter. Rosie's studying singing," she confided to Bob. "She wants to get into the movies."

"But how interesting!" cried Bob enthusiastically, as he rose and shook hands with the future Lady Hamilton.

"Maybe you could give her some advice," said the doting grandmother.

"I'd be only too happy . . ."

"Fetch another chair, Rosie."

The girl raised her eyelids and gave Bob a brief but intense look. "Unless you don't mind sitting in the kitchen," she said.

"Of course not!"

They vanished together into the inner room. Looking out of the window, I saw that the buttes were again in shadow. The rat-lizards had closed their eyes and were shamming death—but only to lull their victim into a sense of false security.

"It's more than luck," Mrs. Coulton was saying, "it's Providence. A big shot in the movies coming here, just when Rosie needs a helping hand."

"Just when movies are going to fold up like vaudeville," said the leprechaun without raising his eyes from the page before him.

"What makes you say those things?"

"It's not me that says them," the old man answered. "It's that Goldwyn guy."

From the kitchen came the sound of a startlingly childish laugh. Bob was evidently making headway. I foresaw another trip to Acapulco, with consequences even more disastrous than the first.

Innocently the procuress, Mrs. Coulton smiled with pleasure.

"I like your friend," she said. "Gets on well with kids. None of that stuffed shirt business."

I accepted the implied rebuke without comment and asked her again if she had known that Mr. Tallis was interested in movies.

She nodded. Yes, he'd told her that he was sending something to one of the Studios. He wanted to make some money. Not for himself; for though he'd lost most of what he once had, there was still enough to live on. No, he wanted some extra money to send to Europe. He'd been married to a German girl, way back, before the First World War. Then they'd been divorced and she had stayed on in Germany with the baby. And now there wasn't anybody left but a granddaughter. Mr. Tallis wanted to bring her over here; but the people at Washington wouldn't let him. So the next best thing was to send her a lot of money so she could eat properly and finish her education. That was why he'd written that thing for the movies.

Her words suddenly reminded me of something in Tallis's script—something about children in postwar Europe prostituting themselves for bars of chocolate. The granddaughter—had she perhaps been one of those children? "*Ich* give you *Schokolade, du* give me *Liebe*. Understand?" They understood only too well. One Hershey bar now; two more afterward.

"What happened to the wife?" I asked. "And the granddaughter's parents?"

"They passed on," said Mrs. Coulton. "I guess they were Jewish, or something."

"Mind you," said the leprechaun suddenly, "I don't have anything against Jews. But all the same . . ." He paused. "Maybe Hitler wasn't so dumb after all."

This time, I could see, it was to the Katzenjammer Kids that he returned.

Another peal of childish laughter broke out in the kitchen. Lady Hamilton at sixteen sounded as though she were about eleven. And yet how mature, how technically perfect had been the look with which she greeted Bob! Obviously, the most disquieting fact about Rosie was that she was simultaneously innocent and knowing, a calculating adventuress and a pigtailed schoolgirl.

"He married again," the old lady went on, ignoring both the giggle and the anti-Semitism. "Someone on the stage. He told me the name, but I've forgotten it. Anyhow it didn't last long. She went off with some other fellow. I say it served him right for going off with her when he had a wife back there in Germany. I don't think it's right, all this divorcing and marrying somebody else's husband."

In the ensuing silence I fabricated a whole biography for this man I had never seen. The young New Englander of good family. Carefully educated, but not to the point of pedantry. Naturally gifted, but not so overwhelmingly as to make him wish to exchange a life of leisure for the fatigues of professional authorship. From Harvard he had gone on to Europe, had lived gracefully, had known the best people everywhere. And then—in Munich, I felt sure—he had fallen in love. I visualized the girl, wearing the German equivalent of Liberty dresses—the daughter of some successful artist or patron of the arts. One of those almost disembodied, those as it were floating products of Wilhelmine wealth and culture; a being at once vague and intense, fascinatingly unpredictable and maddeningly idealistic, *tief* and German. Tallis had fallen in love, had married, had fathered a child in spite of his wife's frigidity, had been almost asphyxiated by the oppressive soulfulness of the domestic atmosphere. How fresh and healthy, by comparison, had seemed the air of Paris and the personal ambience of that young Broadway actress whom he had met vacationing there!

> *La belle Américaine,*
> *Qui rend les hommes fous,*
> *Dans deux ou trois semaines*
> *Partira pour Corfou.*

But this one didn't leave for Corfu—or if she did, it was in Tallis's company. And she wasn't frigid, she didn't float, she was neither vague, nor intense, neither deep, nor soulful, nor an art snob. What she *was*, unfortunately, was a bit of a bitch. And that bit had grown larger with the passage of the years. By the time he divorced her, it had become the entire animal.

Looking back from the vantage point of 1947, the Tallis of my imagination could see precisely what he had done: for the sake of a physical pleasure and the simultaneous excitement and satisfaction of an erotic imagination, he had condemned a wife and a daughter to death at the hands of maniacs, and a granddaughter to the caresses of any soldier or black marketeer with a pocketful of sweetmeats or the price of a decent meal.

Romantic fancies! I turned to Mrs. Coulton.

"Well, I wish I'd known him," I said.

"You'd have liked him," she assured me. "We all liked Mr. Tallis. I'll tell you something," she confided. "Every time I make the trip to Lancaster for the Ladies' Bridge Club, I go to the cemetery, just to visit with him."

"And I bet he hates it," said the leprechaun.

"Now, Elmer," his wife protested.

"But I heard him say it," Mr. Coulton insisted. "Time and again. 'If I die here,' he says, 'I want to be buried out in the desert.'"

"He wrote as much in that script he sent to the Studio," I said.

"He did?" Mrs. Coulton's tone was one of incredulity.

"Yes, he even describes the grave he meant to be buried in. All by itself, under a Joshua tree."

"I could have told him it wasn't legal," said the leprechaun. "Not since the morticians lobbied that bill through the legislature at Sacramento. I knew a man that had to be dug up twenty years after he was buried—way out there behind the buttes." He waved a hand in the direction of Goya's saurian rats. "It cost his nephew three hundred dollars by the time he was all through."

He chuckled at the recollection.

"*I* wouldn't want to be buried in the desert," said his wife emphatically.

"Why not?"

"Too lonely," she answered. "I'd hate it."

While I was wondering what to say next, the pale young mother came down the stairs carrying a diaper. She stopped for a moment to look in at the kitchen.

"Listen, Rosie," she said in a low, angry voice, "It's time you did some work for a change."

Then she turned and walked towards the entrance lobby, where an open door revealed the modern conveniences of that indoor bathroom.

"He's got diarrhea again," she said bitterly, as she passed her grandmother.

Flushed, her eyes bright with excitement, the future

Lady Hamilton emerged from the kitchen. Behind her, in the doorway, stood the future Hamilton, busily imagining that he was going to be Lord Nelson.

"Grandma," the girl announced, "Mr. Briggs thinks he can arrange for me to have a screen test."

The idiot! I got up.

"Time we were going, Bob," I said, knowing that it was already too late.

From the half-open door of the bathroom came the squelchy sound of diapers being rinsed in the toilet bowl.

"Listen!" I whispered to Bob as we passed.

"Listen to what?" he asked.

I shrugged my shoulders. Ears have they, neither do they hear.

Well, that was the nearest we ever got to Tallis in the flesh. In what follows the reader can discover the reflection of his mind. I print the text of "Ape and Essence" as I found it, without change and without comment.

THE SCRIPT

TITLES, credits and finally, to the accompaniment of trumpets and a chorus of triumphant angels, the name of the PRODUCER.

The music changes its character, and if Debussy were alive to write it, how delicate it would be, how aristocratic, how flawlessly pure of all Wagnerian lubricity and bumptiousness, all Straussian vulgarity! For here on the screen, in something better than Technicolor, it is the hour before sunrise. Night seems to linger in the darkness of an almost unruffled sea; but from the fringes of the sky a transparent pallor mounts from green through deepening blue to the zenith. In the east the morning star is still visible.

NARRATOR

Beauty inexpressible, peace beyond understanding...
But, alas, on our screen
This emblem of an emblem
Will probably look like
Mrs. Somebody's illustration
To a poem by Ella
Wheeler Wilcox.
Out of the sublime in Nature
Art all too often manufactures

Only the ludicrous.
But the risk must be run;
For you there, you in the audience,
Somehow and at any price,
Wilcox or worse,
Somehow you must be reminded
Be induced to remember,
Be implored to be willing to
Understand what's What.

As the Narrator speaks, we fade out of our emblem of an emblem of Eternity into the interior of a picture palace filled to capacity. The light grows a little less dim and suddenly we become aware that the audience is composed entirely of well-dressed baboons of both sexes and of all ages from first to second childhood.

NARRATOR

But man, proud man,
Drest in a little brief authority—
Most ignorant of what he is most assur'd.
His glassy essence—like an angry ape,
Plays such fantastic tricks before high heaven
As make the angels weep.

Cut to the screen, at which the apes are so attentively gazing. In a setting such as only Semiramis or Metro-Goldwyn-Mayer could have imagined we see a bosomy young female baboon, in a shell-pink evening gown, her mouth painted purple, her muzzle powdered mauve, her fiery red eyes ringed with mascara. Swaying as voluptuously as the shortness of her hind legs will permit her to do, she walks onto the brightly illuminated stage of a night club and, to the clapping of two or three hundred pairs of hairy hands, ap-

proaches the Louis XV microphone. Behind her, on
all fours and secured by a light steel chain attached
to a dog collar, comes Michael Faraday.

NARRATOR

"Most ignorant of what he is most assur'd . . ." And
I need hardly add that what we call knowledge is
merely another form of Ignorance—highly organized,
of course, and eminently scientific, but for that very
reason all the more complete, all the more productive
of angry apes. When Ignorance was merely ignorance,
we were the equivalents of lemurs, marmosets and
howler monkeys. Today, thanks to that Higher Ignorance which is our knowledge, man's stature has increased to such an extent that the least among us is
now a baboon, the greatest an orangutan or even, if
he takes rank as a Saviour of Society, a true Gorilla.

Meanwhile the baboon-girl has reached the microphone. Turning her head, she catches sight of Faraday
on his knees, in the act of straightening his bent and
aching back.

"Down, sir, down!"

The tone is peremptory; she gives the old man a
cut with her coral-headed riding switch. Faraday
winces and obeys, the apes in the audience laugh de-
lightedly. She blows them a kiss, then, drawing the
microphone toward her, she bares her formidable
teeth and starts to sing, in an expiring bedroom contralto, the latest popular success.

Love, Love, Love—
Love's the very essence
Of everything I think, of everything I do.
Give me, Give me, Give me,

Give me detumescence.

That means you.

Close-up of Faraday's face, as it registers astonishment, disgust, indignation and, finally, such shame and anguish that tears begin to flow down the furrowed cheeks.

Montage shots of the Folks in Radio Land, listening in.

A stout baboon housewife frying sausages, while the loudspeaker brings her the imaginary fulfillment and real exacerbation of her most unavowable wishes.

A baboon baby standing up in its cot, reaching over to the portable on the commode and dialing the promise of detumescence.

A middle-aged baboon financier, interrupting his reading of the stock market news to listen, with closed eyes and a smile of ecstasy. Give me, give me, give me, give me.

Two baboon teen-agers, fumbling to music in a parked car. *"That mean you-ou."* Close-up of mouths and paws.

Cut back to Faraday's tears. The singer turns, catches sight of his agonized face, utters a cry of rage and starts to beat him, blow after savage blow, while the audience applauds tumultuously. The gold and jasper walls of the night club evaporate and for a moment we see the figures of the ape and her captive intellect silhouetted against the dawning twilight of our first sequence. Then these too fade out, and there is only the emblem of an emblem of Eternity.

NARRATOR

The sea, the bright planet, the boundless crystal of the sky—surely you remember them! Surely! Or can it be that you have forgotten, that you have never even discovered what lies beyond the mental Zoo and the inner Asylum and all that Broadway of imaginary theaters, in which the only name in lights is always your own?

The Camera moves across the sky, and now the black serrated shape of a rocky island breaks the line of the horizon. Sailing past the island is a large, four-masted schooner. We approach, we see that the ship flies the flag of New Zealand and is named the *Canterbury*. Her captain and a group of passengers are at the rail, staring intently toward the east. We look through their binoculars and discover a line of barren coast. Then, almost suddenly, the sun comes up behind the silhouette of distant mountains.

NARRATOR

This new bright day is the twentieth of February, 2108, and these men and women are members of the New Zealand Rediscovery Expedition to North America. Spared by the belligerents of the Third World War—not, I need hardly say, for any humanitarian reason, but simply because, like Equatorial Africa, it was too remote to be worth anybody's while to obliterate—New Zealand survived and even modestly flourished in an isolation which, because of the dangerously radioactive condition of the rest of the world, remained for more than a century almost absolute. Now that the danger is over, here come its first explorers, rediscovering America from the West. And meanwhile, on the other side of the world, the black men have been working their way down the Nile and across the Mediterranean. What splendid tribal dances in the bat-infested halls of the Mother of Parliaments!

And the labyrinth of the Vatican—what a capital place in which to celebrate the lingering and complex rites of female circumcision! We all get precisely what we ask for.

The scene darkens; there is a noise of gunfire. When the lights come up again, there squats Dr. Albert Einstein, on a leash, behind a group of baboons in uniform.

The Camera moves across a narrow no-man's land of rubble, broken trees and corpses, and comes to rest on a second group of animals, wearing different decorations and under another flag, but with the same Dr. Albert Einstein, on an exactly similar string, squatting at the heels of their jack boots. Under the tousled aureole of hair, the good, innocent face wears an expression of pained bewilderment. The Camera travels back and forth from Einstein to Einstein. Close shots of the two identical faces, staring wistfully at each other between the polished leather boots of their respective masters.

On the sound track, the voice, the saxophones and cellos continue to yearn for detumescence.

"Is that you, Albert?" one of the Einsteins hesitantly inquires.

The other slowly nods his head.

"Albert, I'm afraid it is."

Overhead the flags of the opposing armies suddenly begin to stir in the freshening breeze. The colored patterns open out, then fold in again upon themselves, are revealed and once more hidden.

NARRATOR

Vertical stripes, horizontal stripes, noughts and crosses, eagles and hammers. Mere arbitrary signs.

But every reality to which a sign has been attached is thereby made subject to its sign. Goswami and Ali used to live at peace. But I got a flag, you got a flag, all Baboon-God's children got flags. So even Ali and Goswami got flags; and because of the flags it immediately became right and proper for the one with the foreskin to disembowel the one without a foreskin, and for the circumcised to shoot the uncircumcised, rape his wife and roast his children over slow fires.

But, meanwhile, above the bunting float the huge shapes of clouds, and beyond the clouds is that blue void which is an emblem of our glassy Essence, and at the foot of the flagstaff grows the wheat and the emerald green rice and the millet. Bread for the body and bread for the spirit. Our choice is between bread and bunting. And bunting, I need hardly add, is what we have almost unanimously chosen.

The Camera drops from the flags to the Einsteins and passes from the Einsteins to the much-decorated General Staffs in the background. All at once and simultaneously the two Field Marshalissimos shout an order. Immediately, from either side, appear baboon technicians, with fully motorized equipment for releasing aerosols. On the pressure tanks of one army are painted the words, SUPER-TULAREMIA, on those of their opponents, IMPROVED GLANDERS, GUARANTEED 99.44% PURE. Each group of technicians is accompanied by its mascot, Louis Pasteur, on a chain. On the Sound-track there is a reminiscence of the baboon-girl. *Give me, give me, give me, give me detumescence. . . .* Then these voluptuous strains modulate into "Land of Hope and Glory," played by massed brass bands, and sung by a choir of fourteen thousand voices.

NARRATOR

What land, you ask? And I answer,
Any old land.
And the Glory, of course, is the Ape-King's,
As for the Hope—
Bless your little heart, there is no hope,
Only the almost infinite probability
Of consummating suddenly,
Or else by agonizing inches,
The ultimate and irremediable
Detumescence.

Close shot of paws at the stopcocks; then the
Camera draws back. Out of the pressure tanks two
streams of yellow fog start to roll toward one another, sluggishly, across no-man's land.

NARRATOR

Glanders, my friends, Glanders—a disease of horses,
not common among humans. But, never fear, Science
can easily make it universal. And these are its symptoms. Violent pains in all the joints. Pustules over the
whole body. Below the skin hard swellings, which
finally burst and turn into sloughing ulcers. Meanwhile the mucous membrane of the nose becomes
inflamed and exudes a copious discharge of stinking
pus. Ulcers rapidly form within the nostrils and eat
away the surrounding bone and cartilage. From the
nose the infection passes to the eyes, mouth, throat and
bronchial passages. Within three weeks most of the
patients are dead. To see that *all* shall die has been
the task of some of those brilliant young D.Sc's now in
the employ of your government. And not of your

government only: of all the other elected or self-appointed organizers of the world's collective schizophrenia. Biologists, pathologists, physiologists—here they are, after a hard day at the lab, coming home to their families. A hug from the sweet little wife. A romp with the children. A quiet dinner with friends, followed by an evening of chamber music or intelligent conversation about politics or philosophy. Then bed at eleven and the familiar ecstasies of married love. And in the morning, after orange juice and Grapenuts, off they go again to their job of discovering how yet greater numbers of families precisely like their own can be infected with a yet deadlier strain of *bacillus mallei*.

There is another yelp of command from the Marshalissimos. Among the booted apes in charge of either army's supply of Genius there is a violent cracking of whips, a tugging of leashes.

Close shot of the Einsteins as they try to resist.

"No, no . . . I can't."

"I tell you I can't."

"Disloyal!"

"Unpatriotic!"

"Filthy Communist!"

"Stinking bourgeois-Fascist!"

"Red Imperialist!"

"Capitalist-Monopolist!"

"Take that!"

"Take that!"

Kicked, whipped, half throttled, each of the Einsteins is finally dragged toward a kind of sentry box. Inside these boxes are instrument boards with dials, knobs and switches.

NARRATOR

Surely it's obvious.
Doesn't every schoolboy know it?
Ends are ape-chosen; only the means are man's.
Papio's procurer, bursar to baboons,
Reason comes running, eager to ratify;
Comes, a catch-fart, with Philosophy, truckling to
  tyrants;
Comes, a pimp for Prussia, with Hegel's Patent His-
  tory;
Comes with Medicine to administer the Ape-King's
  aphrodisiac;
Comes, rhyming and with Rhetoric, to write his ora-
  tions;
Comes with the Calculus to aim his rockets
Accurately at the orphanage across the ocean;
Comes, having aimed, with incense to impetrate
Our Lady devoutly for a direct hit.

The brass bands give place to the most glutinous
of Wurlitzers, "Land of Hope and Glory" to "Onward, Christian Soldiers." Followed by his very Reverend Dean and Chapter, the Right Reverend, the
Baboon-Bishop of the Bronx advances majestic, his
crozier in his jeweled paw, to pronounce benediction
upon the two Field Marshalissimos and their pa-
triotic proceedings.

NARRATOR

Church and State
Greed and Hate:—
Two Baboon-Persons in one Supreme Gorilla.

OMNES

Amen, amen.

THE BISHOP

In nomine Babuini. . . .

On the sound-track it is all *vox humana* and the angel voices of choristers.

"With the (*dim*) Cross of (*pp*) Jesus, (*ff*) going on before."

Huge paws hoist the Einsteins to their feet and, in a close-up, seize their wrists. Ape-guided, those fingers, which have written equations and played the music of Johann Sebastian Bach, close on the master switches and, with a horrified reluctance, slowly press them down. There is a little click, then a long silence which is broken at last by the voice of the Narrator.

NARRATOR

Even at supersonic speeds the missiles will take an appreciable time to reach their destination. So what do you say, boys, to a spot of breakfast while we're waiting for our Last Judgment!

The apes open their haversacks, throw some bread, a few carrots and two or three lumps of sugar to the Einsteins, then fall to themselves on rum and Bologna sausage.

We dissolve to the deck of the schooner, where the scientists of the Rediscovery Expedition are also breakfasting.

NARRATOR

And these are some of the survivors of that Judgment. Such nice people! And the civilization they represent—that's nice too. Nothing very exciting or spectacular of course. No Parthenons or Sistine Chapels, no Newtons or Mozarts or Shakespeares; but also no Ezzelinos, no Napoleons or Hitlers or Jay Goulds, no Inquisitions or NKVD's, no purges, pogroms or lynchings. No heights or abysses, but plenty of milk for the kids, and a reasonably high average IQ, and everything, in a quiet provincial way, thoroughly cozy and sensible and humane.

One of the men raises his binoculars and peers at the shore, now only a mile or two distant. Suddenly he utters an exclamation of delighted astonishment.

"Look!" He hands the glasses to one of his companions. "On the crest of the hill."

The other looks.

Telescopic shot of low hills. On the highest point of the ridge, three oil derricks stand silhouetted against the sky, like the equipment of a modernized and more efficient Calvary.

"Oil!" cries the second observer excitedly. "And the derricks are still standing."

"Still standing?"

There is general astonishment.

"That means," says old Professor Craigie, the geologist, "that there can't have been much of an explosion hereabouts."

"But you don't have to have explosions," explains his colleague from the Department of Nuclear Physics. "Radioactive gases do the job just as effectively and over much wider areas."

"You seem to forget the bacteria and the viruses," puts in Professor Grampian, the biologist. His tone is that of a man who feels that he has been slighted. His young wife, who is only an anthropologist and so has nothing to contribute to the argument, contents herself with glaring angrily at the physicist.

Athletic in tweeds, but at the same time brightly

intelligent behind her horn-rimmed glasses, Miss Ethel Hook, of the Department of Botany, reminds them that there was, almost certainly, a widespread employment of plant diseases. She turns for confirmation of what she says to her colleague, Dr. Poole, who nods approvingly.

"Diseases of food plants," he says in his professorial manner, "would have a long-range effect hardly less decisive than that produced by fissionable material or artificially induced pandemics. Consider, for example, the potato . . ." *widespread epidemic*

"But why bother about any of this fancy stuff?" bluffly booms the engineer of the party, Dr. Cudworth. "Cut the aqueducts, and it's all over in a week. No drinky, no livey." Delighted by his own joke, he laughs enormously.

Meanwhile Dr. Schneeglock, the psychologist, sits listening with a smile of hardly disguised contempt.

"But why even bother about aqueducts?" he asks. "All you need do is just to threaten your neighbor with any of the weapons of mass destruction. Their own panic will do the rest. Remember what the psychological treatment did to New York, for example. The short-wave broadcasts from overseas, the headlines in the evening papers. And immediately there were eight millions of people trampling one another to death on the bridges and in the tunnels. And the survivors scattered through the countryside, like locusts, like a horde of plague-infected rats. Fouling the water supply. Spreading typhoid and diphtheria and venereal disease. Biting, clawing, looting, murdering, raping. Feeding on dead dogs and the corpses of children. Shot at sight by the farmers, bludgeoned by the police, machine-gunned by the State Guard, strung up by the Vigilantes. And the same thing was happening in Chicago, Detroit, Philadelphia, Washington; in London, in Paris; in Bombay and Shanghai and Tokyo; in Moscow, in Kiev, in Stalingrad; in every capital, every manufacturing center, every port, every railway junction, all over the world. Not a shot had been fired and civilization was already in ruins. Why the soldiers ever found it necessary to use their bombs, I really can't imagine."

NARRATOR

Love casts out fear; but conversely fear casts out love. And not only love. Fear also casts out intelligence, casts out goodness, casts out all thought of beauty and truth. What remains is the dumb or studiedly jocular desperation of one who is aware of the obscene Presence in the corner of the room and knows that the door is locked, that there aren't any windows. And now the thing bears down on him. He feels a hand on his sleeve, smells a stinking breath, as the executioner's assistant leans almost amorously toward him. "Your turn next, brother. Kindly step this way." And in an instant his quiet terror is transmuted into a frenzy as violent as it is futile. There is no longer a man among his fellow men, no longer a rational being speaking articulately to other rational beings; there is only a lacerated animal, screaming and struggling in the trap. For in the end fear casts out even a man's humanity. And fear, my good friends, fear is the very basis and foundation of modern life. Fear of the much touted technology which, while it raises our standard of living, increases the probability of our violently dying. Fear of the science which takes away with one hand even more than what it so profusely gives with the other. Fear of the demonstrably fatal institutions for which, in our suicidal loyalty, we are ready to kill and die. Fear of the Great Men whom we have raised, by popular acclaim, to a power which they use, inevitably, to murder and enslave us. Fear of the War we don't want and yet do everything we can to bring about.

As the Narrator speaks, we dissolve to the alfresco picnic of the baboons and their captive Einsteins. They eat and drink, with gusto, while the first two bars of "Onward Christian Soldiers" are repeated again and again, faster and faster, louder and louder. Suddenly the music is interrupted by the first of a succession of enormous explosions. Darkness. A long-drawn, deafening noise of crashing, rending, screaming, moaning. Then silence and increasing light, and once again it is the hour before sunrise, with the morning star and the delicate, pure music.

NARRATOR

Beauty inexpressible, peace beyond understanding . . .

Far off, from below the horizon, a column of rosy smoke pushes up into the sky, swells out into the likeness of an enormous toadstool and hangs there, eclipsing the solitary planet.

We dissolve again to the scene of the picnic. The baboons are all dead. Horribly disfigured by burns, the two Einsteins lie side by side under what remains of a flowering apple tree. Not far off a pressure tank is still oozing its Improved Glanders.

FIRST EINSTEIN

It's unjust, it isn't right . . .

SECOND EINSTEIN

We, who never did any harm to anybody;

FIRST EINSTEIN

We, who lived only for Truth.

NARRATOR

And that precisely is why you are dying in the murderous service of baboons. Pascal explained it all more than three hundred years ago. "We make an idol of truth; for truth without charity is not God, but his image and idol, which we must neither love nor worship." You lived for the worship of an idol. But, in the last analysis, the name of every idol is Moloch. So here you are, my friends, here you are.

Stirred by a sudden gust, the stagnant plague-fog noiselessly advances, sends a wreath of pus-colored vapor swirling among the apple blossoms, then descends to engulf the two recumbent figures. A choking scream announces the death, by suicide, of twentieth-century science.

We dissolve to a point on the coast of Southern California, twenty miles or thereabouts due west of Los Angeles. The scientists of the Rediscovery Expedition are in the act of landing from a whaleboat. A huge sewer, shattered where it enters the sea, stands in the background.

NARRATOR

Parthenon, Coliseum—
Glory that was Greece, grandeur etcetera.
And there are all the others—
Thebes and Copan, Arezzo and Ajanta;

Bourges, taking heaven by violence,
And the Holy Wisdom, floating in repose.
But the glory that was Queen Victoria
Remains unquestionably the W.C.;
The grandeur that was Franklin Delano
Is this by far the biggest drainpipe ever—
Dry now and shattered, Ichabod, Ichabod;
And its freight of condoms (irrepressibly buoyant,
Like hope, like concupiscence) no longer whitens
This lonely beach with a galaxy as of windflowers
Or summer daisies.

strong appetite i. e. sexual drive

Meanwhile the scientists, with Dr. Craigie at their
head, have crossed the beach, scrambled up the low
cliff and are making their way across the sandy and
eroded plain toward the oil wells on the hills beyond.

The Camera holds on Dr. Poole, the Chief Botanist of the Expedition. Like a browsing sheep, he
moves from plant to plant, examining flowers through
his magnifying glass, putting away specimens in his
collecting box, making notes in a little black book.

NARRATOR

Well, here he is, our hero, Dr. Alfred Poole D.Sc.
Better known to his students and younger colleagues
as Stagnant Poole. And the nickname, alas, is painfully
apt. For though not unhandsome, as you see, though
a Fellow of the Royal Society of New Zealand and
by no means a fool, in the circumstances of practical
life his intelligence seems to be only potential, his
attractiveness no more than latent. It is as though he
lived behind plate glass, could see and be seen, but
never establish contact. And the fault, as Dr. Schneeglock of the Psychology Department is only too ready
to tell you, the fault lies with that devoted and in-

tensely widowed mother of his—that saint, that pillar
of fortitude, that vampire, who still presides at his
breakfast table and with her own hands launders his
silk shirts and sacrificially darns his socks.

Miss Hook now enters the shot—enters it on a
burst of enthusiasm.

"Isn't this exciting, Alfred?" she exclaims.

"Very," says Dr. Poole politely.

"Seeing *Yucca gloriosa* in its native habitat—who
would have imagined that we'd ever get the chance?
And *Artemisia tridentata.*"

"There are still some flowers on the *Artemisia,*"
says Dr. Poole. "Do you notice anything unusual
about them?"

Miss Hook examines them, and shakes her head.

"They're a great deal bigger than what's described
in the old text books," he says in a tone of studiedly
repressed excitement.

"A great deal bigger?" she repeats. Her face lights
up. "Alfred, you don't think . . .?"

Dr. Poole nods.

"I'm ready to bet on it," he says. "Tetraploidy.
Induced by irradiation with gamma rays."

"Oh, Alfred," she cries ecstatically. *set g four feet*

NARRATOR

In her tweeds and her horn-rimmed spectacles
Ethel Hook is one of those extraordinarily wholesome, amazingly efficient and intensely English girls
to whom, unless one is oneself equally wholesome,
equally English and even more efficient, one would
so much rather not be married. Which is probably
why, at thirty-five, Ethel is still without a husband.
Still without a husband—but not, she dares to hope,

for much longer. For though dear Alfred has not yet actually proposed, she knows (and knows that he knows) that his mother's dearest wish is for him to do so—and Alfred is the most dutiful of sons. Besides they have so much in common—botany, the University, the poetry of Wordsworth. She feels confident that before they get back to Auckland it will all be arranged—the simple ceremony with dear old Dr. Trilliams officiating, the honeymoon in the Southern Alps, the return to their sweet little house in Mount Eden, and then after eighteen months, the first baby . . .

Cut to the other members of the expedition, as they toil up the hill toward the oil wells. Professor Craigie, their leader, halts to mop his brow and to take stock of his charges.

"Where's Poole?" he asks. "And Ethel Hook?"

Somebody points and, in a long shot, we see the distant figures of the two botanists.

Cut back to Professor Craigie, who cups his hands around his mouth and shouts. "Poole, Poole!"

"Why don't you leave them to their little romance?" asks the genial Cudworth.

"Romance indeed!" Dr. Schneeglock snorts derisively.

"But she's obviously sweet on him."

"It takes two to make a romance."

"Trust a woman to get her man to pop the question."

"You might as well expect him to commit incest with his mother," says Dr. Schneeglock emphatically.

"Poole!" bellows Professor Craigie once more, and turning to the others, "I don't like people to lag behind," he says in a tone of irritation. "In a strange country . . . You never know."

He renews his shouting.

43

Cut back to Dr. Poole and Miss Hook. They hear the distant call, look up from their tetraploid *Artemisia,* wave their hands and start in pursuit of the others. Suddenly Dr. Poole catches sight of something that makes him cry aloud.

"Look!" He points a forefinger.

"What is it?"

"*Echinocactus hexaedrophorus*—and the most beautiful specimen."

Medium long shot from his viewpoint of a ruined bungalow among the sagebrush. Then a close shot of the cactus growing between two paving stones, near the front door. Cut back to Dr. Poole. From the leather sheath at his belt he draws a long, narrow-bladed trowel.

"You're not going to dig it up?"

His only answer is to walk over to where the cactus is growing and squat down beside it.

"Professor Craigie will be so cross," protests Miss Hook.

"Well then, run ahead and keep him quiet."

She looks at him for a few seconds with an expression of solicitude.

"I hate to leave you alone, Alfred."

"You talk as though I were five years old," he answers irritably. "Go ahead, I tell you."

He turns away and starts to dig.

Miss Hook does not immediately obey, but stands looking at him in silence for a little while longer.

NARRATOR

Tragedy is the farce that involves our sympathies, farce, the tragedy that happens to outsiders. Tweedy and breezy, wholesome and efficient, this object of the easiest kind of satire is also the subject of an Intimate

Journal. What flaming sunsets she has seen and vainly attempted to describe! What velvety and voluptuous summer nights! What lyrically lovely days of spring! And oh, the torrents of feeling, the temptations, the hopes, the passionate throbbing of the heart, the humiliating disappointments! And now, after all these years, after so many committee meetings attended, so many lectures delivered and examination papers corrected, now at last, moving in His mysterious way, God has made her, she feels, responsible for this help-less and unhappy man. And because he is unhappy and helpless, she loves him—not romantically of course, not as she loved that curly-headed scamp who, fifteen years ago, swept her off her feet and then married the daughter of that rich contractor, but genuinely none the less, with a strong, protective tenderness.

"All right," she says at last. "I'll go ahead. But promise you won't be long."

"Of course I won't be long."

She turns and walks away. Dr. Poole looks after her; then, with a sigh of relief at finding himself once more alone, resumes his digging.

NARRATOR

"Never," he is repeating to himself, "Never! What-ever mother may say." For though he respects Miss Hook as a botanist, relies on her as an organizer and admires her as a high-minded person, the idea of being made one flesh with her is as unthinkable as a violation of the Categorical Imperative.

Suddenly, from behind him, three villainous-looking men, black-bearded, dirty and ragged, emerge very quietly from out of the ruins of the house, stand poised for a moment, then throw themselves upon the unsuspecting botanist and, before he can so much as utter a cry, force a gag into his mouth, tie his hands behind his back and drag him down into a gully, out of sight of his companions.

We dissolve to a panoramic view of Southern California from fifty miles up in the stratosphere. As the Camera plummets downward, we hear the Narrator's voice.

sea green
color

NARRATOR

The sea and its clouds, the mountains glaucous-golden,
The valleys full of indigo darkness,
The drought of lion-colored plains,
The rivers of pebbles and white sand.
And in the midst of them the City of the Angels.
Half a million houses,
Five thousand miles of streets,
Fifteen hundred thousand motor vehicles,
And more rubber goods than Akron,
More celluloid than the Soviets,
More Nylons than New Rochelle,
More brassieres than Buffalo,
More deodorants than Denver,
More oranges than anywhere,
With bigger and better girls—
The great Metrollopis of the West.

And now we are only five miles up and it becomes increasingly obvious that the great Metrollopis is a ghost town, that what was once the world's largest oasis is now its greatest agglomeration of ruins in a wasteland. Nothing moves in the streets. Dunes of sand have drifted across the concrete. The avenues of palms and pepper trees have left no trace.

The Camera comes down over a large rectangular

graveyard, lying between the ferro-concrete towers of Hollywood and those of Wilshire Boulevard. We land, pass under an arched gateway, enjoy a trucking shot of mortuary gazebos. A baby pyramid. A Gothic sentry box. A marble sarcophagus surmounted by weeping seraphs. The more than life-size statue of Hedda Boddy—"affectionately known," reads the inscription on the pedestal, "as Public Sweetheart Number One. 'Hitch your wagon to a Star.'" We hitch and move on; and suddenly in the midst of all this desolation, here is a little group of human beings. There are four men, heavily bearded and more than a little dirty, and two young women, all of them busy with shovels in or around an opened grave and all dressed identically in shirts and trousers of tattered homespun. Over these rough garments each wears a small square apron upon which, in scarlet wool, is embroidered the word NO. In addition to the aprons, the girls wear a round patch over either breast and, behind, a pair of somewhat larger patches on the seat of their trousers. Three unequivocal negatives greet us as they approach, two more, by way of Parthian shots, as they recede.

Overseeing the laborers from the roof of an adjacent mausoleum sits a man in his middle forties, tall, powerfully built, with the dark eyes and hawk nose of an Algerian corsair. A black curly beard emphasizes the moistness and redness of his full lips. Somewhat incongruously, he is dressed in a pale gray suit of mid-twentieth-century cut, a little too small for him. When we catch our first sight of him, he is absorbed in the paring of his nails.

Cut back to the gravediggers. One of them, the youngest and handsomest of the men, looks up from his shoveling, glances surreptitiously at the overseer on the roof and, seeing him busy with his nails, turns an intensely concupiscent look on the plump girl who stands, stooped over her spade, beside him. Close shot of the two prohibitory patches. NO and again NO, growing larger and larger the more longingly he looks. Cupped already for the deliciously imagined contact, his hand goes out, tentative, hesitant; then, with a jerk, as conscience abruptly gets the better of temptation, is withdrawn again. Biting his lip, the young man turns away and, with redoubled zeal, addresses himself once more to his digging.

Suddenly a spade strikes something hard. There is a cry of delight, a flurry of concerted activity. A moment later a handsome mahogany coffin is hoisted to the surface of the ground.

"Break it open."

"O.K., Chief."

We hear the creaking and cracking of rent wood.

"Man or woman?"

"Man."

"Fine! Spill him out."

With a yo-heave-ho they tilt the coffin and the corpse rolls out onto the sand. The eldest of the bearded gravediggers kneels down beside it and starts methodically to relieve the thing of its watch and jewelry.

NARRATOR

Thanks to the dry climate and the embalmer's art, what remains of the Managing Director of the Golden Rule Brewing Corporation looks as though it had been buried only yesterday. The cheeks are still pink with the rouge applied by the undertaker for the lying-in-state. Stitched into a perpetual smile, the up-turned corners of the lips impart to the round, crumpet-

in new Testament
the devil

like face the maddeningly enigmatic expression of a Madonna by Boltraffio.

Suddenly the lash of a dogwhip cuts across the shoulders of the kneeling gravedigger. The Camera pulls back to reveal the Chief impending, whip in hand, like the embodiment of divine Vengeance, from the height of his marble Sinai.

"Give back that ring."

"Which ring?" the man falters.

For answer the Chief administers two or three more cuts with the dog whip.

"No, no—please! Ow! I'll give it back. Stop!"

The culprit inserts two fingers into his mouth and after a little fumbling draws forth the handsome diamond ring which the deceased brewer bought for himself, when business was so hearteningly good during the Second World War.

"Put it there with the other things," commands the Chief and, as the man obeys, "Twenty-five lashes," he continues with grim relish, "that's what *you're* going to get this evening."

Blubbering, the man begs for indulgence—just for this once. Seeing that tomorrow is Belial Day . . . And after all he's old, he has worked faithfully all his life, has risen to the rank of a Deputy Supervisor. . . .

The Chief cuts him short.

"This is a Democracy," he says. "We're all equal before the Law. And the Law says that everything belongs to the Proletariat—in other words, it all goes to the State. And what's the penalty for robbing the State?" The man looks up at him in speechless misery. "What's the penalty?" the Chief bellows, raising his whip.

in old Testament, personification of wickedness as an evil force

"Twenty-five lashes," comes the almost inaudible reply.

"Good! Well, that settles that, doesn't it? And now what are the clothes like?"

The younger and slimmer of the girls bends down and fingers the corpse's double-breasted black jacket.

"Nice stuff," she says. "And no stains. He hasn't leaked or anything."

"I'll try them on," says the Chief.

With some difficulty they divest the cadaver of its trousers, coat and shirt, then drop it back into the grave and shovel the earth back over its one-piece undergarment. Meanwhile the Chief takes the clothes, sniffs at them critically, then doffs the pearl-gray jacket which once belonged to the Production Manager of Western-Shakespeare Pictures Incorporated, and slips his arms into the more conservative tailoring that goes with malt liquors and the Golden Rule.

NARRATOR

Put yourself in his place. You may not know it, but a complete scribbler, or first card-engine, consists of a breast, or small swift, and two swifts, with the accompanying workers, strippers, fancies, doffers, etc. And if you don't have any carding machinery or power looms, if you don't have any electric motors to run them, or any dynamos to generate the electricity, or any turbines to turn the dynamos, or any coal to raise steam, or any blast furnaces to make steel—why then, obviously, you must depend for your fine cloth on the cemeteries of those who once enjoyed these advantages. And so long as the radioactivity persisted, there weren't even any cemeteries to exploit. For three generations the dwindling remnant of those who survived the consummation of technological progress

lived precariously in the wilderness. It is only during
the last thirty years that it has been safe for them
to enjoy the buried remains of *le confort moderne.*

Close shot of the Chief, grotesque in the borrowed
jacket of a man whose arms were much shorter and
whose belly was much larger than his own. The sound
of approaching footsteps makes him turn his head.

In a long shot from his viewpoint we see Dr. Poole,
his hands tied behind his back, trudging wearily
through the sand. Behind him walk his three captors.
Whenever he stumbles or slackens his pace, they
prick him in the rear with needle-sharp yucca leaves
and laugh uproariously to see him wince.

The Chief stares at them in astonished silence as
they approach.

"What in Belial's name?" he brings out at last.

The little party comes to a halt at the foot of the
mausoleum. The three members of Dr. Poole's escort
bow to the Chief and tell their story. They had been
fishing in their coracle off Redondo Beach; had suddenly seen a huge, strange ship coming out of the
mist; had immediately paddled back to shore to escape
detection. From the ruins of an old house they had
watched the strangers land. Thirteen of them. And
then this man had come wandering with a woman
to the very threshold of their hiding place. The woman
had gone away again and, while the man was grubbing
in the dirt with a tiny spade, they had jumped on him
from behind, gagged him, bound him and now had
brought him here for questioning.

There is a long silence, broken finally by the Chief.

"Do you speak English?"

"Yes, I speak English," Dr. Poole stammers.

"Good. Untie him; hoist him up."

They hoist him—so unceremoniously that he lands on all fours at the Chief's feet.

"Are you a priest?"

"A priest?" Dr. Poole echoes in apprehensive astonishment. He shakes his head.

"Then why don't you have a beard?"

"I . . . I shave."

"Oh, then you're not . . ." The Chief passes a finger across Dr. Poole's chin and cheek. "I see, I see. Get up."

Dr. Poole obeys.

"Where do you come from?"

"New Zealand, sir."

Dr. Poole swallows hard, wishes his mouth were less dry, his voice less tremulous with terror.

"New Zealand? Is that far?"

"Very far."

"You came in a big ship? With sails?"

Dr. Poole nods and adopting that lecture-room manner, which is always his refuge when personal contacts threaten to become too difficult, proceeds to explain why they weren't able to cross the Pacific under steam.

"There would have been no place to refuel. It's only for coastwise traffic that our shipping companies are able to make use of steamers."

"Steamers?" the Chief repeats, his face alight with interest. "You still have steamers? But that must mean you didn't have the Thing?"

Dr. Poole looks puzzled.

"I don't quite catch your meaning," he says. "What thing?"

"*The* Thing. You know—when He took over."

Raising his hands to his forehead, he makes the sign of the horns with extended forefingers. Devoutly, his subjects follow suit.

"You mean the Devil?" says Dr. Poole dubiously.
The other nods.
"But, but . . . I mean, *really* . . ."

NARRATOR

Our friend is a good Congregationalist, but, alas,
on the liberal side. Which means that he has never
given the Prince of this world his ontological due. To
put it brutally, he doesn't believe in Him.

"Yes, He got control," the Chief explains. "He won
the battle and took possession of everybody. That was
when they did all this."

With a wide, comprehensive gesture he takes in the
desolation that was once Los Angeles. Dr. Poole's expression brightens with understanding.

"Oh, I see. You mean the Third World War. No,
we were lucky; we got off without a scratch. Owing
to its peculiar geographical situation," he adds profes-
sorially, "New Zealand was of no strategic importance
to . . ."

The Chief cuts short a promising lecture.

"Then you've still got trains?" he questions.

"Yes, we've still got trains," Dr. Poole answers, a
little irritably. "But, as I was saying . . ."

"And the engines really work?"

"Of course they work. As I was saying . . ."

Startlingly the Chief lets out a whoop of delight and
claps him on the shoulder.

"Then you can help us to get it all going again.
Like in the good old days before . . ." He makes the
sign of horns. "We'll have trains, real trains." And in
an ecstasy of joyous anticipation, he draws Dr. Poole
toward him, puts an arm round his neck and kisses
him on both cheeks.

53

Shrinking with an embarrassment that is reinforced by disgust (for the great man seldom washes and is horribly foul-mouthed) Dr. Poole disengages himself.

"But I'm not an engineer," he protests. "I'm a botanist."

"What's that?"

"A botanist is a man who knows about plants."

"War plants?" the Chief asks hopefully.

"No, no, just plants. Things with leaves and stalks and flowers—though of course," he adds hastily, "one mustn't forget the cryptogams. And as a matter of fact the cryptogams are my special pets. New Zealand, as you probably know, is particularly rich in cryptogams . . ."

"But what about the engines?"

"Engines?" Dr. Poole repeats contemptuously. "I tell you, I don't know the difference between a steam turbine and a diesel."

"Then you can't do anything to help us get the trains running again?"

"Not a thing."

Without a word the Chief raises his right leg, places his foot against the pit of Dr. Poole's stomach, then sharply straightens the bent knee.

Close shot of Dr. Poole, as he raises himself, shaken and bruised, but with no bones broken, from the heap of sand onto which he has fallen. Over the shot we hear the Chief shouting to his retainers.

Medium shot of the gravediggers and fishermen, as they come running in response to the summons.

The Chief points down at Dr. Poole.

"Bury him."

"Alive or dead?" asks the plumper of the girls in her rich contralto voice.

The Chief looks down at her. Shot from his viewpoint. With an effort he turns away. His lips move. He is repeating the relevant passage from the Shorter Catechism. "What is the nature of woman? Answer: Woman is the vessel of the Unholy Spirit, the source of all deformity, the enemy of the race, the . . ."

"Alive or dead?" the plump girl repeats.

The Chief shrugs his shoulders.

"As you like," he answers with studied indifference.

The plump girl claps her hands.

"Goody, goody!" she cries and turns to her companions. "Come on, boys. Let's have some fun."

They close in on Dr. Poole, lift him screaming from the ground and drop him feet first into the half-filled grave of the Managing Director of the Golden Rule Brewing Corporation. While the plump girl holds him down, the men shovel the loose dry earth into place. In a very short time he is buried up to the waist.

On the sound track the victim's screams and the excited laughter of the executioners taper off into a silence that is broken by the voice of the Narrator.

NARRATOR

Cruelty and compassion come with the chromosomes;
All men are merciful and all are murderers.
Doting on dogs, they build their Dachaus;
Fire whole cities and fondle the orphans;
Are loud against lynching, but all for Oakridge;
Full of future philanthropy, but today the NKVD.
Whom shall we persecute, for whom feel pity?
It is all a matter of the moment's mores,
Of words on wood pulp, of radios roaring,
Of Communist kindergartens or first communions.

Only in the knowledge of his own Essence
Has any man ceased to be many monkeys.

The laughter and the pleas for mercy return to the
sound track. Then, suddenly, we hear the Chief.

"Stand back," he shouts. "I can't see."

They obey. In silence the Chief looks down at Dr.
Poole.

"You know all about plants," he says at last. "Why
don't you grow some roots down there?"

The sally is greeted by enormous guffaws.

"Why don't you put out some nice little pink
flowers?"

We are shown a close-up of the botanist's agonized
face.

"Mercy, mercy . . ."

The voice breaks, grotesquely; there is another burst
of hilarity.

"I could be useful to you. I could show you how
to get better crops. You'd have more to eat."

"More to eat?" the Chief repeats with sudden interest. Then he frowns savagely. "You're lying!"

"I'm not. I swear by Almighty God."

There is a murmur of shocked protest.

"He may be almighty in New Zealand," says the
Chief. "But not here—not since the Thing happened."

"But I know I can help you."

"Are you ready to swear by Belial?"

Dr. Poole's father was a clergyman and he himself
is a regular churchgoer; but it is with heartfelt fervor
that he does what is asked of him.

"By Belial. I swear by Almighty Belial."

Everyone makes the sign of the horns. There is a
long silence.

"Dig him up."

"Oh, Chief," the plump girl protests. "That isn't fair!"

"Dig him up, you vessel of Unholiness!"

His tone carries immediate conviction; they dig with such fervor that in less than a minute Dr. Poole is out of his grave and standing rather unsteadily, at the foot of the mausoleum.

"Thank you," he manages to say; then his knees give way and he collapses.

There is a chorus of contemptuously good-humored laughter.

The Chief leans from his marble perch. "Here, you there, the red-headed vessel." He hands the girl a bottle. "Make him drink some of this," he orders. "He's got to be able to walk. We're going back to Headquarters."

She sits down beside Dr. Poole, raises his limp body, props the wobbling head against the interdictions on her bosom, and administers the restorative.

Dissolve to a street. Four of the bearded men are carrying the Chief in a litter. The others straggle behind, moving slowly through the drifted sand. Here and there, under the porches of ruined filling stations, in the gaping doorways of office buildings, lie heaps of human bones.

Medium close shot of Dr. Poole. Still holding the bottle in his right hand, he walks a little unsteadily, singing "Annie Laurie" to himself, with intense feeling. Drunk on an empty stomach—the empty stomach, moreover, of a man whose mother has always had conscientious objections to alcohol—the strong red wine has taken prompt effect.

> "And for bonny Annie Laurie
> I'd lay me doon and dee . . ."

57

In the middle of the final phrase, the two girl grave-diggers enter the shot. Approaching the singer from behind, the plump one gives him a friendly slap on the back. Dr. Poole starts, turns around, and looks suddenly apprehensive. But her smile is reassuring.

"I'm Flossie," she says. "And I hope you're not cross with me because I wanted to bury you?"

"Oh, no, no, not a bit," Dr. Poole assures her in the tone of one who says he has no objection to the young lady lighting a cigarette.

"It's not that I had anything against you," Flossie assures him.

"Of course not."

"I just wanted a laugh, that's all."

"Quite, quite."

"People look so screamingly funny when they're being buried."

"Screamingly," Dr. Poole agrees, and forces a nervous giggle.

Feeling the need for more courage, he fortifies himself with another swig from the bottle.

"Well, see you later," says the plump girl. "I've got to go and talk to the Chief about lengthening the sleeves of his new jacket."

She gives him another slap on the back and hurries away.

Dr. Poole is left alone with her companion. He steals a glance at her. She is eighteen; she has red hair and dimples, a charming face and a slender adolescent body.

"My name's Loola," she volunteers. "What's yours?"

"Alfred," Dr. Poole replies. "My mother was a great admirer of *In Memoriam*," he adds by way of explanation.

"Alfred," the red-headed girl repeats. "I shall call

you Alfie. I'll tell you something, Alfie: I don't really like these public burials. I don't know why I should be different from other people, but they don't make me laugh. I can't see anything funny about them."

"I'm glad to hear it," says Dr. Poole.

"You know, Alfie," she resumes, after a little silence, "you're really a very lucky man."

"Lucky?"

Loola nods.

"First of all you're dug up—and I've never seen *that* happen before—and now you walk straight into the Purification Ceremonies."

"Purification Ceremonies?"

"Yes, it's Belial Day tomorrow—Belial Day," she insists in response to the blank look of incomprehension on the other's face. "Don't tell me you don't know what happens on Belial Eve."

Dr. Poole shakes his head.

"But when do *you* have your Purification?"

"Well, we take a bath every day," says Dr. Poole, who has just been reminded, yet once more, that Loola most decidedly doesn't.

"No, no," she says impatiently. "I mean the Purification of the Race."

"Of the Race?"

"Hell, your priests don't let the deformed babies go on living, do they?"

There is a silence; then Dr. Poole counters with a question of his own.

"Are there many deformed babies born here?"

She nods affirmatively.

"Ever since the Thing—ever since He's been in charge."

She makes the sign of the horns. "They say that before that, there weren't any."

59

"Did anyone ever tell you about the effect of gamma rays?"

"Gamma rays? What's a gamma ray?"

"It's the reason for all those deformed children."

"You're not trying to suggest that it wasn't Belial, are you?" Her tone is one of indignant suspicion; she looks at him as St. Dominic might have eyed an Albigensian heretic.

"No, no, of course not," Dr. Poole hastens to assure her. "He's the primary cause—that goes without saying." Clumsily and inexpertly, he makes the sign of the horns. "I was merely suggesting the nature of the secondary causes—the means He used to carry out His . . . His providential purpose, if you see what I mean."

His words and, still more, his pious gesture allay Loola's suspicions. Her face clears; she gives him her most charming smile. The dimples in her cheeks come to life like a pair of adorable little creatures fitfully leading a secret and autonomous existence in independence of the rest of Loola's face. Dr. Poole returns her smile, but almost instantly looks away, blushing as he does so to the roots of his hair.

NARRATOR

Out of the enormity of his respect for his mother, our poor friend here is still, at thirty-eight, a bachelor. Too full of an unnatural piety to marry, he has spent half a lifetime surreptitiously burning. Feeling that it would be a sacrilege to ask a virtuous young gentlewoman to share his bed, he inhabits, under the carapace of academic respectability, a hot and furtive world, where erotic phantasies beget an agonizing repentance and adolescent desires forever struggle with the maternal precepts. And now here is Loola—Loola without the least pretension to education or good breeding, Loola *au naturel* with a musky redolence which, on second thought, has something really rather fascinating about it. What wonder if he reddens and (against his will, for he longs to go on looking at her) averts his eyes.

For consolation and in hope of an accession of boldness, he resorts again to the bottle. Suddenly the boulevard narrows to a mere footpath between two dunes of sand.

"After you," says Dr. Poole, politely bowing.

She smiles her acknowledgment of a courtesy, to which, in this place where men take precedence and the vessels of the Unholy Spirit follow after, she is wholly unaccustomed.

Trucking shot, from Dr. Poole's viewpoint, of Loola's back. NO NO, NO NO, NO NO, step after step in undulant alternation. Cut back to a close shot of Dr. Poole, gazing, wide-eyed, and from Dr. Poole's face once again to Loola's back.

NARRATOR

It is the emblem, outward, visible, tangible, of his own inner consciousness. Principle at odds with concupiscence, his mother and the Seventh Commandment superimposed upon his fancies and the facts of Life.

The dunes subside. Once more the road is wide enough for two to walk abreast. Dr. Poole steals a glance at his companion's face and sees it clouded with an expression of melancholy.

"What is it?" he asks solicitously and, greatly daring, adds "Loola" and lays a hand on her arm.

"It's terrible," she says in a tone of quiet despair.

"What's terrible?"

"Everything. You don't want to think about those things; but you're one of the unlucky ones—you can't help thinking about them. And you almost go crazy. Thinking and thinking about someone, and wanting and wanting. And you know you mustn't. And you're scared to death of what they might do if they found out. But you'd give everything in the world just for five minutes, to be free for five minutes. But no, no, no. And you clench your fists and hold yourself in—and it's like tearing yourself to pieces. And then suddenly, after all that suffering, suddenly . . ." she breaks off.

"Suddenly what?" inquires Dr. Poole.

She looks at him sharply, but sees on his face only an expression of inquiring and genuinely innocent incomprehension.

"I can't make you out," she says at last. "Is it true, what you told the Chief? You know, about your not being a priest."

All at once she blushes.

"If you don't believe me," says Dr. Poole with wine-begotten gallantry, "I'm ready to prove it."

She looks at him for a moment, then shakes her head and, in a kind of terror, turns away. Nervously she smooths her apron.

"And meanwhile," he continues, emboldened by her new-found shyness, "you haven't told me just what it is that suddenly happens."

Loola glances about her to make sure that nobody is within earshot, then speaks at last almost in a whisper.

"Suddenly He starts to take possession of everybody. For weeks he makes them think about those things— and it's against the Law, it's wicked. The men get so mad, they start hitting you and calling you a vessel, the way the priests do."

"A vessel?"

She nods.

"Vessel of the Unholy Spirit."

"Oh, I see."

"And then comes Belial Day," she goes on after a little pause. "And then . . . well, you know what that means. And afterwards, if you have a baby, the chances are that He'll punish you for what He has made you do." She shudders, then makes the sign of the horns. "I know we have to accept what He wills," she adds. "But oh, I do so hope that, if ever I have any babies, they'll be all right."

"But of course they'll be all right," cries Dr. Poole. "After all, there isn't anything wrong about *you*."

Delighted by his own audacity, he looks down at her.

Close shot from his viewpoint. NO NO NO, NO NO NO . . .

Mournfully, Loola shakes her head.

"That's where you're wrong," she says. "I've got an extra pair of nipples."

"Oh," says Dr. Poole in a tone which makes us realize that the thought of his mother has momentarily obliterated the effects of the red wine.

"Not that there's anything really bad about that," Loola hastily adds. "Even the best people have them. It's perfectly legal. They allow you up to three pairs. And seven toes and fingers. Anything over that gets liquidated at the Purification. My friend Polly—*she* had a baby this season. Her first one. And it's got four pairs, and no thumbs. There isn't any chance for it. In fact it's been condemned already. She's had her head shaved."

"Had her head shaved?"

"They do it to all the girls whose babies are liquidated."

"But why?"

Loola shrugs her shoulders.

"Just to remind them that He's the Enemy."

NARRATOR

"To put it," as Schroedinger has said, "drastically,
though perhaps a little naïvely, the injuriousness of
a marriage between first cousins might very well be
increased by the fact that their grandmother had
served for a long period as an X-ray nurse. It is not
a point that need worry any individual personally. But
any possibility of gradually infecting the human race
with unwanted latent mutations ought to be a matter
of concern to the community." It ought to be; but,
needless to say, it isn't. Oakridge is working three
shifts a day; an atomic power plant is going up on the
coast of Cumberland; and on the other side of the
fence, goodness only knows what Kapitza is up to on
the top of Mount Ararat, what surprises that wonder-
ful Russian Soul, about which Dostoevsky used to
write so lyrically, has in store for Russian bodies and
the carcasses of Capitalists and Social Democrats.

Once again sand bars the road. They enter another
winding pathway between the dunes and are suddenly
alone, as though in the middle of the Sahara.

Trucking shot from Dr. Poole's viewpoint. NO NO,
NO NO . . . Loola halts and turns back toward him. NO
NO NO. The Camera moves up to her face and all at
once he notices that its expression is tragical.

NARRATOR

The Seventh Commandment, the Facts of Life. But there is also another Fact, to which one cannot react by a mere departmentalized negation or a no less fragmentary display of lust—the Fact of Personality.

"I don't want them to cut my hair," she says in a breaking voice.

"But they won't."

"They will."

"They can't, they mustn't." Then, amazed by his own daring, he adds, "It's much too beautiful."

Still tragic, Loola shakes her head.

"I feel it," she says, "in my bones. I just *know* it'll have more than seven fingers. They'll kill it, they'll cut my hair off, they'll whip me—and He *makes* us do those things."

"What things?"

She looks at him for a moment without speaking; then, with an expression almost of terror, drops her eyes.

"It's because He *wants* us to be miserable."

Covering her face with her hands, she starts to sob uncontrollably.

NARRATOR

The wine within and, without, the musky reminder
Of those so near, warm, ripe, orby and all but
Edible Facts of Life . . . And now her tears, her
 tears . . .

Dr. Poole takes the girl in his arms and, while she sobs against his shoulder, strokes her hair with all the tenderness of the normal male he has momentarily become.

"Don't cry," he whispers, "don't cry. It'll be all right. I'll always be there. I won't let them do anything to you."

She permits herself gradually to be comforted. The sobbing becomes less violent and finally ceases altogether. She looks up and the smile she gives him through her tears is so unequivocally amorous that anyone but Dr. Poole would have accepted the invitation forthwith. The seconds pass and, while he is still hesitating, her expression changes, she drops her eyelids over an avowal that she suddenly feels to have been too frank, and turns away.

"I'm sorry," she murmurs, and starts to rub away her tears with the knuckles of a hand that is as grubby as a child's.

Dr. Poole takes out his handkerchief and tenderly wipes her eyes.

"You're so sweet," she says. "Not a bit like the men here."

She smiles up at him again. Like a pair of enchanting little wild animals emerging from concealment, out come the dimples.

So impulsively that he has no time to feel surprise at what he is doing, Dr. Poole takes her face between his hands and kisses her on the mouth.

Loola resists for a moment, then abandons herself in a surrender so complete as to be more active than his assault.

On the sound track "Give me detumescence" modulates into *Liebestod* from *Tristan*.

Suddenly Loola stiffens into a shuddering rigidity. Pushing him away, she stares up wildly into his face; then turns and glances over her shoulder with an expression of guilty terror.

"Loola!"

He tries to draw her close again, but she breaks away from him and starts to run along the narrow path.

NO NO, NO NO, NO NO. . . .

We dissolve to the corner of Fifth Street and Pershing Square. As of old, the Square is the hub and center of the city's cultural life. From a shallow well in front of the Philharmonic Auditorium two women are drawing water in a goatskin, which they empty into earthenware jars for other women to carry away. From a bar slung between two rusty lamp posts hangs the carcass of a newly slaughtered ox. Standing in a cloud of flies, a man with a knife is cleaning out the entrails.

"That looks good," says the Chief genially.

The butcher grins and, with bloody fingers, makes the sign of the horns.

A few yards away stand the communal ovens. The Chief orders a halt, and graciously accepts a piece of the newly baked bread. While he is eating, ten or twelve small boys enter the shot, staggering under inordinate loads of fuel from the nearby Public Library. They tumble their burdens onto the ground and, stimulated by the blows and curses of their elders, hurry back for more. One of the bakers opens a furnace door and starts to shovel the books into the flames.

All the scholar in Dr. Poole, all the bibliophile, is outraged by the spectacle.

"But this is frightful!" he protests.

The Chief only laughs.

"In goes *The Phenomenology of Spirit*, out comes the corn bread. And damned good bread it is."

He takes another bite.

Meanwhile Dr. Poole has bent down and, from the very brink of destruction, has snatched to safety a charming little duodecimo Shelley.

"Thank G——" he begins, but fortunately remembers where he is and manages to check himself in time.

He slips the volume into his pocket and, turning to the Chief, "But what about culture?" he asks. "What about the social inheritance of humanity's painfully acquired wisdom? What about the best that has been thought and . . ."

"They can't read," the Chief answers with his mouth full. "No, that's not quite true. We teach all of them to read *that*."

He points. Medium shot from his viewpoint of Loola—Loola with dimples and all the rest, but also with the large red NO on her apron, the two smaller NO's on her shirt front.

"That's all the book learning they need. And now," he commands his bearers, "move on."

Trucking shot of the litter as it is carried through the doorless entrance of what was once the Biltmore Coffee Shop. Here, in the malodorous twilight, twenty or thirty women, some middle-aged, some young, some mere girls, are busily weaving on primitive looms of the kind used by the Indians of Central America.

"None of these vessels had a baby this season," the Chief explains to Dr. Poole. He frowns and shakes his head. "When they're not producing monsters, they're sterile. What we're going to do for manpower, Belial only knows . . ."

They advance further into the Coffee Shop, pass a group of three- and four-year-old children under the supervision of an aged vessel with a cleft palate and fourteen fingers and come to a halt under an archway giving access to a second dining room only slightly smaller than the first.

Over the shot we hear the sound of a chorus of youthful voices reciting in unison the opening phrases of the Shorter Catechism.

"Question: What is the chief end of Man? Answer: The chief end of Man is to propitiate Belial, deprecate His enmity and avoid destruction for as long as possible."

Cut to a close shot of Dr. Poole's face, on which we see an expression of amazement mingled with a growing horror. Then a long long shot from his viewpoint. In five rows of twelve, sixty boys and girls between the ages of thirteen and fifteen stand rigidly at attention, gabbling as fast as they can in a shrill harsh monotone. Facing them, on a dais, sits a small, fat man wearing a long robe of black and white goatskins and a fur cap with a stiff leather edging, to which are attached two medium-sized horns. Beardless and sallow, his face shines with a profuse perspiration, which he is forever wiping away with the hairy sleeve of his cassock.

Cut back to the Chief, as he leans down and touches Dr. Poole on the shoulder.

"That," he whispers, "is our leading Satanic Science Practitioner. I tell you, he's an absolute whizz at Malicious Animal Magnetism."

Over the shot we hear the mindless gabble of the children.

"Question: To what fate is Man predestined? Answer: Belial has, out of his mere good pleasure, from all eternity elected all now living to everlasting perdition."

"Why does he wear horns?" asks Dr. Poole.

"He's an Archimandrite," the Chief explains. "Due for his third horn any time now."

Cut to a medium shot of the dais.

"Excellent," the Satanic Science Practitioner is saying in a high piping voice, like the voice of an extraordinarily priggish and self-satisfied small boy. "Excellent!" He wipes his forehead. "And now tell me why you deserve everlasting perdition."

There is a moment's silence. Then, in a chorus that starts a little raggedly, but soon swells to a loud unanimity, the children answer.

"Belial has perverted and corrupted us in all the parts of our being. Therefore, we are, merely on account of that corruption, deservedly condemned by Belial."

Their teacher nods approvingly.

"Such," he squeaks unctuously, "is the inscrutable justice of the Lord of Flies."

"Amen," respond the children.

All make the sign of the horns.

"And what about your duty towards your neighbor?"

"My duty towards my neighbor," comes the choral answer, "is to do my best to prevent him from doing unto me what I should like to do unto him; to subject myself to all my governors; to keep my body in absolute chastity, except during the two weeks following Belial Day; and to do my duty in that state of life to which it hath pleased Belial to condemn me."

"What is the Church?"

"The Church is the body of which Belial is the head and all possessed people are the members."

"Very good," says the Practitioner, wiping his face yet once more. "And now I need a young vessel."

He runs his eyes over the ranks of his pupils, then points a finger.

"You there. Third from the left in the second row ... The vessel with the yellow hair. Come here."

Cut back to the group around the litter.

The bearers are grinning with happy anticipation and, looking intensely red and moist and fleshy among the black curls of the mustache and beard, even the Chief's full lips are curved into a smile. But there is no smile on Loola's face. Pale, her hand over her mouth, her eyes wide and staring, she is watching the proceedings with the horror of one who has been through this kind of ordeal herself. Dr. Poole glances at her, then back at the victim, whom we now see, from his viewpoint, slowly advancing toward the dais.

"Up here," squeaks the almost babyish voice in a tone of authority. "Stand by me. Now face the class."

The child does as she is told.

Medium close shot of a tall slender girl of fifteen with the face of a Nordic madonna. NO, proclaims the apron attached to the waistband of her ragged pedal pushers; NO, NO, the patches over her budding breasts.

The Practitioner points at her accusingly.

"Look at it," he says, wrinkling up his face into a grimace of disgust. "Did you ever see anything so revolting?"

He turns to the class.

"Boys," he squeaks. "Any of you who feels any Malicious Animal Magnetism coming out of this vessel, hold up your hand."

Cut to a long shot of the class. Without exception, all the boys are holding up their hands. Their faces wear that expression of lustful and malevolent amusement, with which the orthodox have always looked

71

on, while their spiritual pastors torment the hereditary scapegoats or still more severely punish the heretics who threaten the interest of the Establishment.

Cut back to the Practitioner. He sighs hypocritically and shakes his head.

"I feared as much," he says. Then he turns to the girl beside him on the dais. "Now tell me," he says, "what is the Nature of Woman?"

"The Nature of Woman?" the child repeats unsteadily.

"Yes, the Nature of Woman. Hurry up!"

She glances at him with an expression of terror in her blue eyes, then turns away. Her face becomes deathly pale. Her lips tremble; she swallows hard.

"Woman," she begins, "woman . . ."

Her voice breaks, her eyes overflow with tears; in a desperate effort to control her feelings she clenches her fists and bites her lip.

"Go on!" the Practitioner shrilly shouts. And picking up a willow switch from the floor, he gives the child a sharp cut across the calves of her bare legs. "Go on!"

"Woman," the girl begins once more, "is the vessel of the Unholy Spirit, the source of all deformity, the . . . the . . . Owl"

She winces under another blow.

The Science Practitioner laughs and the whole class follows suit.

"The enemy . . ." he prompts.

"Oh, yes—the enemy of the race, punished by Belial and calling down punishment on all those who succumb to Belial in her."

There is a long silence.

"Well," says the Practitioner at last, "that's what

you are. That's what all vessels are. And now go, go!"
he squeals and with sudden fury he strikes at her again
and again.

Crying with pain, the child jumps down from the
dais and runs back to her place in the ranks.

Cut back to the Chief. His brow is wrinkled in a
frown of displeasure.

"All this progressive education!" he says to Dr. Poole.
"No proper discipline. I don't know what we're coming
to. Why, when I was a boy, our old Practitioner used
to tie them over a bench and go to work with a birch
rod. 'That'll teach you to be a vessel,' he'd say, and
then swish, swish, swish! Belial, how they howled!
That's what *I* call education. Well, I've had enough
of this," he adds. "Quick march!"

As the litter moves out of the shot, the Camera
holds on Loola who remains, staring in an agony of
fellow feeling at the tear-wet face and heaving shoulders of the little victim in the second row. A hand
touches her arm. She starts, turns apprehensively and
is relieved to find herself looking into the kindly face
of Dr. Poole.

"I entirely agree with you," he whispers. "It's wrong,
it's unjust."

Only after she has thrown a quick look over her
shoulder does Loola venture to give him a little smile
of gratitude.

"Now we must go," she says.

They hurry after the others. Following the litter,
they retrace their steps through the Coffee Shop, then
turn to the right and enter the Cocktail Bar. At one
end of the room an enormous pile of human bones
reaches almost to the ceiling. Squatting on the floor,
in a thick white dust, a score of craftsmen are engaged
in fashioning drinking cups out of skulls, knitting

needles from ulnas, flutes and recorders from the
longer shank bones, ladles, shoe horns and dominoes
from pelvises, and spigots out of femurs.

A halt is called, and, while one of the workmen
plays "Give me Detumescence" on a shinbone flute,
another presents the Chief with a superb necklace
of graded vertebrae ranging in size from a baby's
cervicals to the lumbars of a heavyweight boxer.

NARRATOR

"And he set me down in the midst of the valley
that was full of bones; and lo, they were very dry."
The dry bones of some of those who died, by thousands, by millions, in the course of those three bright
summer days that, for you there, are still in the
future. "And he said unto me, Son of man, can these
bones live?" The answer, I replied, is in the negative.
For though Baruch might save us (perhaps) from
taking our places in such an ossuary as this, he can
do nothing to avert that other, slower, nastier death. . . .

Trucking shot of the litter as it is carried up the
steps into the main lobby. Here the stink is overpow-
ering, the filth beyond description. Close-up of two
rats gnawing at a mutton bone, of the flies on the
purulent eyelids of a small girl. The Camera pulls
back for a longer shot. Forty or fifty women, half of
them with shaven heads, are sitting on the stairs,
among the refuse on the floor, on the tattered remnants
of ancient beds and sofas. Each of them is nursing a
baby, all the babies are ten weeks old, and all those
belonging to shaven mothers are deformed. Over close-
ups of little faces with hare lips, little trunks with
stumps instead of legs and arms, little hands with
clusters of supernumerary fingers, little bodies adorned

74

with a double row of nipples, we hear the voice of the
Narrator.

NARRATOR

For this other death—not by plague, this time, not by
poison, not by fire, not by artificially induced cancer,
but by the squalid disintegration of the very substance
of the species—this gruesome and infinitely unheroic
death-in-birth could as well be the product of atomic
industry as of atomic war. For in a world powered by
nuclear fission everybody's grandmother would have
been an X-ray technician. And not only everybody's
grandmother—everybody's grandfather and father and
mother as well, everybody's ancestors back to three
and four and five generations of them that hate Me.

From the last of the deformed babies the Camera
pulls back to Dr. Poole who is standing, his handkerchief held to his still too sensitive nose, staring
with horrified bewilderment at the scene around him.

"All the babies look as if they were exactly the
same age," he says, turning to Loola, who is still beside him.

"Well, what do you expect? Seeing that practically
all of them were born between the tenth and the
seventeenth of December."

"But that must mean that . . ." He breaks off, deeply
embarrassed. "I think," he concludes hastily, "that
things must be rather different here from what they
are in New Zealand. . . ."

In spite of the wine, he remembers his gray-haired
mother across the Pacific and, blushing guiltily, coughs
and averts his eyes.

"There's Polly," cries his companion, and hurries
across the room.

Mumbling apologies as he picks his way between the squatting or recumbent mothers, Dr. Poole follows her.

Polly is sitting on a straw-filled sack near what was once the Cashier's desk. She is a girl of eighteen or nineteen, small and fragile, her head shaved like that of a criminal prepared for execution. She has a face whose beauty is all in the fine bones and the big luminous eyes. It is with an expression of hurt bewilderment that those eyes now look up into Loola's face and from Loola's face move without curiosity, almost without comprehension, to that of the stranger who accompanies her.

"Darling!"

Loola bends down to kiss her friend. NO NO, from Dr. Poole's viewpoint. Then she sits down beside Polly and puts a comforting arm around her. Polly hides her face against the other's shoulder and both girls begin to cry. As though infected by their grief, the little monster in Polly's arms wakes up and utters a thin complaining howl. Polly raises her head from her friend's shoulder and, her face still wet with tears, looks down at the deformed child, then opens her shirt and pushing aside one of the crimson NO's, gives it the breast. With an almost frantic hunger the child starts to suck.

"I love him," Polly sobs. "I don't want them to kill him."

"Darling," is all that Loola can find to say, "darling!"

A loud voice interrupts her.

"Silence there! Silence!"

Other voices take up the refrain.

"Silence!"

"Silence there!"

"Silence, silence!"

76

In the lobby all talk ceases abruptly and there is a long, expectant hush. Then a horn is blown and another of those strangely babyish, but self-important voices announces: "His Eminence the Arch-Vicar of Belial, Lord of the Earth, Primate of California, Servant of the Proletariat, Bishop of Hollywood."

Long shot of the hotel's main staircase. Dressed in a long robe of Anglo-Nubian goatskins and wearing a golden crown set with four tall, sharp horns, the Arch-Vicar is seen majestically descending. An acolyte holds a large goatskin umbrella over his head and he is followed by twenty or thirty ecclesiastical dignitaries, ranging in rank from three-horned Patriarchs to one-horned Presbyters and hornless Postulants. All of them, from the Arch-Vicar downward, are conspicuously beardless, sweaty and fat-rumped and, when any of them speaks, it is always in a fluting contralto.

The Chief rises from his litter and advances to meet the incarnation of spiritual authority.

NARRATOR

female voice of lowest range

Church and State,
Greed and Hate:—
Two baboon-persons
In one Supreme Gorilla.

The Chief inclines his head respectfully. The Arch-Vicar raises his hands to his tiara, touches the two anterior horns, then lays his spiritually charged fingertips on the Chief's forehead.

"May you never be impaled upon His Horns."

"Amen," says the Chief; then straightening himself up and changing his tone abruptly from the devout to the briskly businesslike, "Everything OK for tonight?" he asks.

77

In the voice of a ten-year-old, but with the long-winded and polysyllabic unctuousness of a veteran ecclesiastic, long accustomed to playing the role of a superior being set apart from and above his fellows, the Arch-Vicar replies that all things are in order. Under the personal supervision of the Three-Horned Inquisitor and the Patriarch of Pasadena, a devoted band of Familiars and Postulants has traveled from settlement to settlement, making the yearly census. Every mother of a monster has been marked down. Heads have been shaved and the preliminary whippings administered. By this time all the guilty have been transported to one or other of the three Purification Centers at Riverside, San Diego and Los Angeles. The knives and the consecrated bull's pizzles have been made ready and, Belial willing, the ceremonies will begin at the appointed hour. Before tomorrow's sunrise the purification of the land should be complete.

Once more the Arch-Vicar makes the sign of the horns, then stands for a few seconds in recollected silence. Reopening his eyes, he turns to the ecclesiastics in his train.

"Go, take the shaven ones," he squeaks, "take these defiled vessels, these living testimonies of Belial's enmity, and lead them to the place of their shame."

A dozen Presbyters and Postulants hurry down the stairs and out into the crowd of mothers.

"Hurry, hurry!"

"In Belial's name."

Slowly, reluctantly, the crop-headed women rise to their feet. Their little burdens of deformity pressed against bosoms heavy with milk, they move toward the door in a silence more painfully expressive of misery than any outcry.

Medium shot of Polly on her sack of straw. A young

78

Postulant approaches and pulls her roughly to her feet.

"Up!" he shouts in a voice of an angry and malevolent child. "Get up, you spawner of filth!"

And he slaps her across the face. Cringing away from a second blow, Polly almost runs to rejoin her fellow victims near the entrance.

Dissolve to a night sky, with stars between thin bars of cloud and a waning moon already low in the West. There is a long silence; then we begin to hear the sound of distant chanting. Gradually it becomes articulate in the words, "Glory to Belial, to Belial in the lowest," repeated again and again.

NARRATOR

An inch from the eyes the ape's black paw
Eclipses the stars, the moon, and even
Space itself. Five stinking fingers
Are all the World.

The silhouette of a baboon's hand advances toward the Camera, grows larger and more menacing, and finally engulfs everything in blackness.

We cut to the interior of the Los Angeles Coliseum. By the smoky and intermittent light of torches we see the faces of a great congregation. Tier above tier, like massed gargoyles, spouting the groundless faith, the subhuman excitement, the collective imbecility which are the products of ceremonial religion—spouting them from black eyeholes, from quivering nostrils, from parted lips, while the chanting monotonously continues: "Glory to Belial, to Belial in the lowest." Below, in the arena, hundreds of shaven girls and women, each with her tiny monster in her arms, are kneeling before the steps of the High Altar. Awe-inspiring in their chasubles of Anglo-Nubian fur, in their tiaras of gilded horns, Patriarchs and Archimandrites, Presbyters and Postulants stand in two groups at the head of the altar steps, chanting antiphonally in a high treble to the music of bone recorders and a battery of xylophones.

SEMICHORUS I

Glory to Belial,

SEMICHORUS II

To Belial in the lowest!

Then, after a pause, the music of the chant changes and a new phase of the service begins.

SEMICHORUS I

It is a terrible thing,

SEMICHORUS II

Terrible terrible,

SEMICHORUS I

To fall into the hands,

SEMICHORUS II

The huge hands and the hairy,

SEMICHORUS I

Into the hands of living Evil,

SEMICHORUS II

Hallelujah!

SEMICHORUS I

Into the hands of the Enemy of man,

SEMICHORUS II

Our boon companions;

SEMICHORUS I

Of the Rebel against the Order of Things—

SEMICHORUS II

And we have conspired with him against ourselves;

SEMICHORUS I

Of the great Blowfly who is the Lord of Flies,

SEMICHORUS II

Crawling in the heart;

SEMICHORUS I

Of the naked Worm that never dies,

SEMICHORUS II

And, never dying, is the source of our eternal life;

SEMICHORUS I

Of the Prince of the Powers of the Air—

SEMICHORUS II

Spitfire and Stuka, Beelzebub and Azazel, Hallelujah!

SEMICHORUS I

Of the Lord of this world;

SEMICHORUS II

And its defiler;

SEMICHORUS I

Of the great Lord Moloch,

SEMICHORUS II

Patron of all nations;

SEMICHORUS I

Of Mammon our master,

SEMICHORUS II

Omnipresent:

SEMICHORUS I

Of Lucifer the all-powerful,

SEMICHORUS II

In Church, in State;

SEMICHORUS I

Of Belial,

SEMICHORUS II

Transcendent,

SEMICHORUS I

Yet, oh, how immanent

ALL TOGETHER

Of Belial, Belial, Belial, Belial.

As the chanting dies away, two hornless Postulants descend, seize the nearest of the shaven women, raise her to her feet and lead her up, dumb with terror, to where, at the head of the altar steps, the Patriarch of Pasadena stands whetting the blade of

a long butcher's knife. The thickset Mexican mother
stands staring at him in fascinated horror, open-
mouthed. Then one of the Postulants takes the child
out of her arms and holds it up before the Patriarch.

Close shot of a characteristic product of progressive
technology—a harelipped, Mongolian idiot. Over the
shot we hear the chanting of the Chorus.

SEMICHORUS I

I show you the sign of Belial's enmity,

SEMICHORUS II

Foul, foul;

SEMICHORUS I

I show you the fruit of Belial's grace,

SEMICHORUS II

Filth infused in filth.

SEMICHORUS I

I show you the penalty for obedience to His Will,

SEMICHORUS II

On earth as it is in Hell.

SEMICHORUS I

Who is the Breeder of all deformities?

SEMICHORUS II

Mother.

SEMICHORUS I

Who is the chosen vessel of Unholiness?

SEMICHORUS II

Mother.

SEMICHORUS I

And the curse that is on our race?

SEMICHORUS II

Mother.

SEMICHORUS I

Possessed, possessed—

SEMICHORUS II

Inwardly, outwardly:

SEMICHORUS I

Her incubus an object, her subject a succubus—

SEMICHORUS II

And both are Belial;

SEMICHORUS I

Possessed by the Blowfly.

SEMICHORUS II

Crawling and stinging,

SEMICHORUS I

Possessed by that which irresistibly

SEMICHORUS II

Goads her, drives her,

SEMICHORUS I

Like the soiled fitchew,

SEMICHORUS II

Like the sow in her season,

SEMICHORUS I

Down a steep place

SEMICHORUS II

Into filth unutterable;

SEMICHORUS I

Whence, after much wallowing,

SEMICHORUS II

After many long draughts of the swill,

SEMICHORUS I

Mother emerging, nine months later,

SEMICHORUS II

Bears this monstrous mockery of a man.

SEMICHORUS I

How then shall there be atonement?

SEMICHORUS II

By blood.

SEMICHORUS I

How shall Belial be propitiated?

SEMICHORUS II

Only by blood.

The Camera moves from the altar to where, tier above tier, the pale gargoyles stare down in hungry anticipation at the scene below. And suddenly the faces open their black mouths and start to chant in unison, hesitantly at first, then with growing confidence and ever greater volume of sound.

"Blood, blood, blood, the blood, the blood, blood, blood, the blood . . ."

We cut back to the altar. The sound of the mindless, subhuman chanting continues monotonously over the shot.

The Patriarch hands his whetstone to one of the attendant Archimandrites, and then with his left hand takes the deformed child by the neck and impales it on his knife. It utters two or three little bleating cries, and is silent.

The Patriarch turns, allows half a pint of blood to spill out on the altar, then tosses the tiny corpse into the darkness beyond. The chanting rises in a savage crescendo. "Blood, blood, the blood, the blood, blood, blood, the blood . . ."

"Drive her away!" cries the Patriarch in a commanding squeak.

In terror the mother turns and hurries down the steps. The two Postulants follow, striking at her savagely with their consecrated bulls' pizzles. The chanting is punctuated by piercing screams. From the congregation comes a noise that is half commiserating groan, half grunt of satisfaction. Flushed and a little breathless from so unusually strenuous an exercise, the plump young Postulants seize another woman—a girl this time, frail and slender almost to the point of childishness. Her face is hidden as they drag her up the steps. Then one of them steps back a little and we recognize Polly.

Thumbless, eight-nippled, the child is held up before the Patriarch.

SEMICHORUS I

Foul, foul! How shall there be atonement?

SEMICHORUS II

By blood.

SEMICHORUS I

How shall Belial be propitiated?

This time it is the entire congregation that answers. "Only by blood, blood, blood, blood, the blood . . ."

The Patriarch's left hand closes about the infant's neck.

"No, no, don't. Please!"

Polly makes a movement toward him, but is held back by the Postulants. Very deliberately, while she sobs, the Patriarch impales the child on his knife, then tosses the body into the darkness behind the altar.

There is a loud cry. We cut to a medium close shot of Dr. Poole. Conspicuous in his front-row seat, he has fainted.

Dissolve to the interior of the Unholy of Unholies. The shrine, which stands at one end of the arena's shorter axis, to the side of the high altar, is a small oblong chamber of adobe brick, with an altar at one end and, at the other, sliding doors, closed at present, except for a gap at the center through which one can see what is going on in the arena. On a couch in the center of the shrine reclines the Arch-Vicar. Not far off a hornless Postulant is frying pig's trotters over a charcoal brazier, and near him a two-horned Archimandrite is doing his best to revive Dr. Poole, who lies inanimate on a stretcher. Cold water and two or three sharp slaps in the face at last produce the desired result. The botanist sighs, opens his eyes, wards off another slap and sits up.

"Where am I?" he asks.

"In the Unholy of Unholies," the Archimandrite answers, "And there is his Eminence."

Dr. Poole recognizes the great man and has enough presence of mind to incline his head respectfully.

"Bring a stool," commands the Arch-Vicar.

The stool is brought. He beckons to Dr. Poole, who scrambles to his feet, walks a little unsteadily across the room and sits down. As he does so a particularly loud shriek makes him turn his head.

Long shot, from his viewpoint, of the High Altar. The Patriarch is in the act of tossing yet another little monster into the darkness, while his acolytes shower blows upon its screaming mother.

Cut back to Dr. Poole, who shudders and covers his face with his hands. Over the shot we hear the monotonous chanting of the congregation. "Blood, blood, blood."

"Horrible!" says Dr. Poole, "Horrible!"

"And yet there's blood in your religion too," remarks the Arch-Vicar, smiling ironically. " 'Washed in the blood of the Lamb.' Isn't that correct?"

"Perfectly correct," Dr. Poole admits. "But we don't actually do the washing. We only talk about it—or, more often, we only sing about it, in hymns."

Dr. Poole averts his eyes. There is a silence. At this moment the Postulant approaches with a large platter, which, together with a couple of bottles, he sets down on a table beside the couch. Spearing one of the trotters with a genuine antique twentieth-century forgery of an early Georgian fork, the Arch-Vicar starts to gnaw.

"Help yourself," he squeaks between two bites.

"And here's some wine," he adds, indicating one of the bottles.

Dr. Poole, who is extremely hungry, obeys with alacrity and there is another silence, loud with the noise of eating and the chant of the blood.

"You don't believe it, of course," says the Arch-Vicar at last, with his mouth full.

"But I assure you . . ." Dr. Poole protests.

His zeal to conform is excessive, and the other holds up a plumb, pork-greasy hand.

"Now, now, now! But I'd like you to know that we have good reasons for believing as we do. Ours, my dear sir, is a rational and realistic faith." There is a pause while he takes a swig from the bottle and helps himself to another trotter. "I take it that you're familiar with world history?"

"Purely as a dilettante," Dr. Poole answers modestly. But he thinks he can say that he has read most of the more obvious books on the subject—Graves's *Rise and Extinction of Russia*, for example; Basedow's *Collapse of Western Civilization*; Bright's inimitable *Europe, an Autopsy*; and, it goes without saying, that absolutely delightful and, though it's only a novel, that genuinely veracious book, *The Last Days of Coney Island* by dear old Percival Pott. "You know it, of course?"

The Arch-Vicar shakes his head.

"I don't know anything that's been published after the Thing," he answers curtly.

"But how stupid of me!" cries Dr. Poole, regretting, as so often in the past, that gushing loquacity with which he overcompensates a shyness that, left to itself, would reduce him almost to speechlessness.

"But I've read quite a bit of the stuff that came out before," the Arch-Vicar continues. "They had some pretty good libraries here in Southern California. Mined out now, for the most part. In future, I'm afraid, we'll have to go further afield for our fuel. But meanwhile we've baked our bread and I've managed to save three or four thousand volumes for our Seminary."

"Like the Church in the Dark Ages," says Dr. Poole with cultured enthusiasm. "Civilization has no better friend than religion. That's what my agnostic friends will never . . ." Suddenly remembering that the tenets of that Church were not quite the same as those professed by this, he breaks off and, to hide his embarrassment, takes a long pull at his bottle.

But fortunately the Arch-Vicar is too much preoccupied with his own ideas to take offense at the *faux pas* or even to notice it.

"As I read history," he says, "it's like this. Man pitting himself against Nature, the Ego against the Order of Things, Belial" (a perfunctory sign of the horns) "against the Other One. For a hundred thousand years or so the battle's entirely indecisive. Then, three centuries ago, almost overnight the tide starts to run uninterruptedly in one direction. Have another of these pig's feet, won't you?"

Dr. Poole helps himself to his second, while the other begins his third.

"Slowly at first, then with gathering momentum, man begins to make headway against the Order of Things." The Arch-Vicar pauses for a moment to spit out a piece of cartilage. "With more and more of the human race falling into line behind him, the Lord of Flies, who is also the Blowfly in every individual heart, inaugurates his triumphal march across a world, of which he will so soon become the undisputed Master."

Carried away by his own shrill eloquence and forgetting for a moment that he is not in the pulpit of St. Azazel's, the Arch-Vicar makes a sweeping gesture. The trotter falls off his fork. With a good-humored laugh at his own expense, he picks it up from the floor, wipes it on the sleeve of his goat-skin cassock, takes another bite and continues.

"It began with machines and the first grain ships from the New World. Food for the hungry and a burden lifted from men's shoulders. 'Oh God, we thank Thee for all the blessings which in Thy Bounty . . .' Etcetera etcetera." The Arch-Vicar laughs derisively. "Needless to say nobody ever gets anything for nothing. God's bounties have their price, and Belial always sees that it's a stiff one. Take those machines, for example. Belial knew perfectly well that, in finding a little alleviation from toil, flesh would be subordinated to iron and mind would be made the slave of wheels. He knew that if a machine is foolproof, it must also be skillproof, talentproof, inspirationproof. Your money back if the product should be faulty, and twice your money back if you can find in it the smallest trace of genius or individuality! And then there was that good food from the New World. 'Oh God, we thank Thee . . .' But Belial knew that feeding means breeding. In the old days, when people made love, they merely increased the infantile mortality rate and lowered the expectation of life. But after the coming of the food ships, it was different. Copulation resulted in population—with a vengeance!"

Once again the Arch-Vicar utters his shrill laugh.

Dissolve to a shot through a powerful microscope of spermatozoa frantically struggling to reach their Final End, the vast moonlike ovum in the top left-hand corner of the slide. On the sound track we hear the tenor voice in the last movement of Liszt's Faust Symphony: *La femme éternelle toujours nous élève. La femme éternelle toujours* . . . Cut to an aerial view of London in 1800. Then back to the Darwinian race for survival and self-perpetuation. Then to a view of London in 1900—and again to the spermatozoa—and again to London, as the German airmen saw it in 1940. Dissolve to a close shot of the Arch-Vicar.

"'Oh God,'" he intones in the slightly tremulous voice that is always considered appropriate to such utterances, "'we thank Thee for all these immortal souls.'" Then, changing his tone, "These immortal souls," he goes on, "lodged in bodies that grow progressively sicklier, scabbier, scrubbier, year after year, as all the things foreseen by Belial inevitably come to pass. The overcrowding of the planet. Five hundred, eight hundred, sometimes as many as two thousand people to a square mile of food-producing land—and the land in process of being ruined by bad farming. Everywhere erosion, everywhere the leaching out of minerals. And the deserts spreading, the forests dwindling. Even in America, even in that New World, which was once the hope of the Old. Up goes the spiral of industry, down goes the spiral of soil fertility. Bigger and better, richer and more powerful—and then almost suddenly, hungrier and hungrier. Yes, Belial foresaw it all—the passage from hunger to imported food, from imported food to booming population and from booming population back to hunger again. Back to hunger. The New Hunger, the Higher Hunger, the hunger of enormous industrialized proletariats, the hunger of city dwellers with money, with all the modern conveniences, with cars and radios and every imaginable gadget, the hunger that is the cause of total wars and the total wars that are the cause of yet more hunger."

The Arch-Vicar pauses to take another swig from his bottle.

"And remember this," he adds: "even without synthetic glanders, even without the atomic bomb, Belial could have achieved all His purposes. A little more slowly, perhaps, but just as surely, men would have destroyed themselves by destroying the world they lived in. They couldn't escape. He had them skewered on both His horns. If they managed to wriggle off the horn of total war, they would find themselves impaled on starvation. And if they were starving, they would be tempted to resort to war. And just in case they should try to find a peaceful and rational way out of their dilemma, He had another subtler horn of self-destruction all ready for them. From the very beginning of the industrial revolution He foresaw that men would be made so over-weeningly bumptious by the miracles of their own technology that they would soon lose all sense of reality. And that's precisely what happened. These wretched slaves of wheels and ledgers began to congratulate themselves on being the Conquerors of Nature. Conquerors of Nature, indeed! In actual fact, of course, they had merely upset the equilibrium of Nature and were about to suffer the consequences. Just consider what they were up to during the century and a half before the Thing. Fouling the rivers, killing off the wild animals, destroying the forests, washing the topsoil into the sea, burning up an ocean of petroleum, squandering the minerals it had taken the whole of geological time to deposit. An orgy of criminal imbecility. And they called it Progress. Progress," he repeats, "Progress! I tell you, that was too rare an invention to have been the product of any merely human mind—too fiendishly ironical! There had to be Outside Help for that. There had to be the Grace of Belial, which, of course, is always forthcoming—that is, for anyone who's prepared to co-operate with it. And who isn't?"

"Who isn't?" Dr. Poole repeats with a giggle; for he feels that he has to make up somehow for his mistake about the Church in the Dark Ages.

"Progress and Nationalism—those were the two great ideas He put into their heads. Progress—the theory that you can get something for nothing; the theory that you can gain in one field without paying for your gain in another; the theory that you alone understand the meaning of history; the theory that you know what's going to happen fifty years from now; the theory that, in the teeth of all experience, you can foresee all the consequences of your present actions; the theory that Utopia lies just ahead and that, since ideal ends justify the most abominable means, it is your privilege and duty to rob, swindle, torture, enslave and murder all those who, in your opinion (which is, by definition, infallible), obstruct the onward march to the earthly paradise. Remember that phrase of Karl Marx's: 'Force is the midwife of Progress.' He might have added—but of course Belial didn't want to let the cat out of the bag at that early stage of the proceedings—that Progress is the midwife of Force. Doubly the midwife, for the fact of technological progress provides people with the instruments of ever more indiscriminate destruction, while the myth of political and moral progress serves as the excuse for using those means to the very limit. I tell you, my dear sir, an undevout historian is mad. The longer you study modern history, the more evidence you find of Belial's

Guiding Hand." The Arch-Vicar makes the sign of
the horns, refreshes himself with another drink of wine,
then continues. "And then there was Nationalism—the
theory that the state you happen to be subject to is
the only true god, and that all other states are false
gods; that all these gods, true as well as false, have
the mentality of juvenile delinquents; and that every
conflict over prestige, power or money is a crusade
for the Good, the True and the Beautiful. The fact
that such theories came, at a given moment of history,
to be universally accepted is the best proof of Belial's
existence, the best proof that at long last He'd won
the battle."

"I don't quite follow," says Dr. Poole.

"But surely it's obvious. Here you have two notions.
Each is intrinsically absurd and each leads to courses
of action that are demonstrably fatal. And yet the
whole of civilized humanity decides, almost suddenly,
to accept these notions as guides to conduct. Why?
And at Whose suggestion, Whose prompting, Whose
inspiration? There can be only one answer."

"You mean, you think it was . . . it was the Devil?"

"Who else desires the degradation and destruction of
the human race?"

"Quite, quite," Dr. Poole agrees. "But all the same
as a Protestant Christian, I really can't . . ."

"Is that so?" says the Arch-Vicar sarcastically. "Then
you know better than Luther, you know better than
the whole Christian Church. Are you aware, sir, that
from the second century onward no orthodox Christian
believed that a man could be possessed by God? He
could only be possessed by the Devil. And why did
people believe that? Because the facts made it impossible for them to believe otherwise. Belial's a fact,
Moloch's a fact, diabolic possession's a fact."

95

"I protest," cries Dr. Poole. "As a man of science . . ."

"As a man of science you're bound to accept the working hypothesis that explains the facts most plausibly. Well, what are the facts? The first is a fact of experience and observation—namely that nobody wants to suffer, wants to be degraded, wants to be maimed or killed. The second is a fact of history—the fact that, at a certain epoch, the overwhelming majority of human beings accepted beliefs and adopted courses of action that could not possibly result in anything but universal suffering, general degradation and wholesale destruction. The only plausible explanation is that they were inspired or possessed by an alien consciousness, a consciousness that willed their undoing and willed it more strongly than they were able to will their own happiness and survival."

There is a silence.

"Of course," Dr. Poole ventures at last to suggest, "those facts could be accounted for in other ways."

"But not so plausibly, not nearly so simply," insists the Arch-Vicar. "And then consider all the other evidence. Take the First World War, for example. If the people and the politicians hadn't been possessed, they'd have listened to Benedict XV or Lord Lansdowne—they'd have come to terms, they'd have negotiated a peace without victory. But they couldn't, they couldn't. It was impossible for them to act in their own self-interest. They had to do what the Belial in them dictated—and the Belial in them wanted the Communist Revolution, wanted the Fascist reaction to that revolution, wanted Mussolini and Hitler and the Politburo, wanted famine, inflation and depression; wanted armaments as a cure for unemployment; wanted the persecution of the Jews and the Kulaks; wanted the Nazis and the Communists to divide

Poland and then go to war with one another. Yes, and He wanted the wholesale revival of slavery in its most brutal form. He wanted forced migrations and mass pauperization. He wanted concentration camps and gas chambers and cremation ovens. He wanted saturation bombing (what a deliciously juicy phrase!). He wanted the destruction overnight of a century's accumulation of wealth and all the potentialities of future prosperity, decency, freedom and culture. Belial wanted all this and, being the Great Blowfly in the hearts of the politicians and generals, the journalists and the Common Man, He was easily able to get the Pope ignored even by Catholics, to have Lansdowne condemned as a bad patriot, almost a traitor. And so the war dragged on for four whole years; and afterward everything went punctually according to Plan. The world situation went steadily from bad to worse, and as it worsened, men and women became progressively more docile to the leadings of the Unholy Spirit. The old beliefs in the value of the individual soul faded away; the old restraints lost their effectiveness; the old compunctions and compassions evaporated. Everything that the Other One had ever put into people's heads oozed out, and the resulting vacuum was filled by the lunatic dreams of Progress and Nationalism. Granted the validity of those dreams, it followed that mere people, living here and now, were no better than ants and bedbugs and might be treated accordingly. And they *were* treated accordingly, they most certainly were!"

The Arch-Vicar chuckles shrilly and helps himself to the last of the trotters.

"For his period," he continues, "old man Hitler was a pretty good specimen of a demoniac. Not so completely possessed, of course, as many of the great na-

97

tional leaders in the years between 1945 and the beginning of the Third World War, but definitely above the average of his own time. More than almost any of his contemporaries, he had a right to say, 'Not I, but Belial in me.' The others were possessed only in spots, only at certain times. Take the scientists, for example. Good, well-meaning men, for the most part. But He got hold of them all the same—got hold of them at the point where they ceased to be human beings and became specialists. Hence, the glanders and those bombs. And then remember that man—what was his name?—the one that was President of the United States for such a long time. . . ."

"Roosevelt?" suggests Dr. Poole.

"That's it—Roosevelt. Well, do you recall that phrase he kept repeating through the whole of the Second World War? 'Unconditional surrender, unconditional surrender.' Plenary inspiration—that's what *that* was. Direct and plenary inspiration!"

"You say so," demurs Dr. Poole. "But what's your proof?"

"The proof?" repeats the Arch-Vicar. "The whole of subsequent history is the proof. Look at what happened when the phrase became a policy and was actually put into practice. Unconditional surrender—how many millions of new cases of tuberculosis? How many millions of children forced to be thieves or prostituting themselves for bars of chocolate? Belial was particularly pleased about the children. And again, unconditional surrender—the ruin of Europe, the chaos in Asia, the starvation everywhere, the revolutions, the tyrannies. Unconditional surrender—and more innocents had to undergo worse suffering than at any other period in history. And, as you know very well, there's nothing that Belial likes better than the suffering of innocents. And finally, of course, there was the Thing. Unconditional surrender and bang!—just as He'd always intended. And it all happened without any miracle or special intervention, merely by natural means. The more one thinks about the workings of His Providence, the more unfathomably marvelous it seems." Devoutly, the Arch-Vicar makes the sign of the horns. There is a little pause. "Listen," he says, holding up his hand.

For a few seconds they sit without speaking. The dim, blurred monotone of the chant swells into audibility. "Blood, blood, blood, the blood . . ." There is a faint cry as yet another little monster is spitted on the Patriarch's knife, then the thudding of bulls' pizzles on flesh and, through the excited roaring of the congregation, a succession of loud, scarcely human screams.

"You'd hardly think he could have produced *us* without a miracle," the Arch-Vicar thoughtfully continues. "But He did, He did. By purely natural means, using human beings and their science as His instruments, He created an entirely new race of men, with deformity in their blood, with squalor all around them and ahead, in the future, no prospects but of more squalor, worse deformity and, finally, complete extinction. Yes, it's a terrible thing to fall into the hands of the Living Evil."

"Then why," asks Dr. Poole, "do you go on worshiping Him?"

"Why do you throw food to a growling tiger? To buy yourself a breathing space. To put off the horror of the inevitable, if only for a few minutes. In earth as it is in Hell—but at least one's still on earth."

"It hardly seems worth while," says Dr. Poole in the philosophical tone of one who has just dined.

Another unusually piercing scream makes him turn his head toward the door. He watches for a while in silence. This time, his expression is one in which horror has been considerably mitigated by scientific curiosity.

"Getting used to it, eh?" says the Arch-Vicar genially.

NARRATOR

Conscience, custom—the first makes cowards,
Makes saints of us sometimes, makes human beings.
The other makes Patriots, Papists, Protestants,
Makes Babbitts, Sadists, Swedes or Slovaks,
Makes killers of Kulaks, chlorinators of Jews,
Makes all who mangle, for lofty motives,
Quivering flesh, without qualm or question
To mar their certainty of Supreme Service.

Yes, my friends, remember how indignant you once felt when the Turks massacred more than the ordinary quota of Armenians, how you thanked God that you lived in a Protestant, progressive country, where such things simply couldn't happen—couldn't happen because men wore bowler hats and traveled daily to town by the eight twenty-three. And then reflect for a moment on a few of the horrors you now take for granted; the outrages against the most rudimentary human decencies that have been perpetrated on your behalf (or perhaps by your own hands); the atrocities you take your little girl to see, twice a week, on the news reel—and she finds them commonplace and boring. Twenty years hence, at this rate, your grandchildren will be turning on their television sets for a look at the gladiatorial games; and, when those begin to pall, there will be the Army's mass crucifixion of Conscientious Objectors or the skinning alive, in full *done after dinner*

color, of the seventy thousand persons suspected, at Tegucigalpa, of un-Honduranean activities.

Meanwhile, in the Unholy of Unholies, Dr. Poole is still looking out through the crack between the sliding doors. The Arch-Vicar is picking his teeth. There is a comfortable, postprandial silence. Suddenly Dr. Poole turns to his companion.

"Something's happening," he cries excitedly. "They're leaving their seats."

"I'd been expecting that for quite a long time now," replies the Arch-Vicar, without ceasing to pick his teeth. "It's the blood that does it. That and, of course, the whipping."

"They're jumping down into the arena," Dr. Poole continues. "They're running after one another. What on earth . . . ? Oh, my God! I beg your pardon," he hastily adds. "But really, *really* . . ."

Much agitated, he walks away from the door.

"There *are* limits," he says.

"That's where you're wrong," replies the Arch-Vicar. "There are no limits. Everybody's capable of anything—but *anything*."

Dr. Poole does not answer. Drawn irresistibly by a force that is stronger than his will, he has returned to his old place and is staring out, avidly and in horror, at what is going on in the arena.

"It's monstrous!" he cries indignantly. "It's utterly revolting."

The Arch-Vicar rises heavily from his couch and, opening a little cupboard in the wall, takes out a pair of binoculars, which he hands to Dr. Poole.

"Try these," he says. "Night glasses. Standard Navy equipment from before the Thing. You'll see everything."

"But you don't imagine . . ."

"Not merely do I imagine," says the Arch-Vicar, with an ironically benignant smile; "I see with my own eyes. Go ahead, man. Look. You've never seen anything like this in New Zealand."

"I certainly have not," says Dr. Poole in the kind of tone his mother might have used.

All the same he finally raises the binoculars to his eyes.

Long shot from his viewpoint. It is a scene of Satyrs and Nymphs, of pursuits and captures, provocative resistances followed by the enthusiastic surrender of lips to bearded lips, of panting bosoms to the impatience of rough hands, the whole accompanied by a babel of shouting, squealing and shrill laughter.

Cut back to the Arch-Vicar, whose face is puckered into a grimace of contemptuous distaste.

"Like cats," he says at last. "Only cats have the decency not to be gregarious in their courting. And you still have doubts about Belial—even after this?"

There is a pause.

"Was this something that happened after . . . after the Thing?" Dr. Poole inquires.

"In two generations."

"Two generations!" Dr. Poole whistles. "Nothing recessive about *that* mutation. And don't they . . . well, I mean, don't they feel like doing this sort of thing at any other season?"

"Just for these five weeks, that's all. And we only permit two weeks of actual mating."

"Why?"

The Arch-Vicar makes the sign of the horns.

"On general principles. They have to be punished for having been punished. It's the Law of Belial. And,

I may say, we really let them have it if they break the rules."

"Quite, quite," says Dr. Poole, remembering with discomfort the episode with Loola among the dunes.

"It's pretty hard for the ones who throw back to the old-style mating pattern."

"Are there many of those?"

"Between five and ten per cent of the population. We call them 'Hots.'"

"And you don't permit . . . ?"

"We beat the hell out of them when we catch them."

"But that's monstrous!"

"Of course it is," the Arch-Vicar agrees. "But remember your history. If you want solidarity, you've got to have either an external enemy or an oppressed minority. We have no external enemies, so we have to make the most of our Hots. They're what the Jews were under Hitler, what the bourgeois were under Lenin and Stalin, what the heretics used to be in Catholic countries and the Papists under the Protestants. If anything goes wrong, it's always the fault of the Hots. I don't know what we'd do without them."

"But don't you ever stop to think what *they* must feel?"

"Why should I? First of all, it's the law. ~~Condign~~ *suitable* punishment for having been punished. Second, if they're discreet, they won't get punished. All they've got to do is to avoid having babies at the wrong season and to disguise the fact that they fall in love and make permanent connections with persons of the opposite sex. And, if they don't want to be discreet, they can always run away."

"Run away? Where to?"

"There's a little community up North, near Fresno.

Eighty-five per cent Hot. It's a dangerous journey, of course. Very little water on the way. And if we catch them, we bury them alive. But if they choose to take the risk, they're perfectly free to do so. And then finally there's the priesthood." He makes the sign of the horns. "Any bright boy, who shows early signs of being a Hot, has his future assured: we make a priest of him."

Several seconds pass before Dr. Poole ventures to ask his next question.

"You mean, you . . . ?"

"Precisely," says the Arch-Vicar. "For the Kingdom of Hell's sake. Not to mention the strictly practical reasons. After all, the business of the community has got to be carried on somehow, and obviously the laity are in no condition to do it."

The noise from the arena swells to a momentary climax.

"Nauseous!" squeaks the Arch-Vicar with a sudden intensification of abhorrence. "And this is nothing to what it will be later on. How thankful I am that I've been preserved from such ignominy! Not they, but the Enemy of Mankind incarnate in their disgusting bodies. Kindly look over there." He draws Dr. Poole toward him; he points a thick forefinger. "To the left of the High Altar—with that little red-headed vessel. That's the Chief. The Chief!" he repeats with derisive emphasis. "What sort of a ruler is *he* going to be during the next two weeks?"

Resisting the temptation to make personal remarks about a man who, though temporarily in retirement, is destined to return to power, Dr. Poole utters a nervous little laugh.

"Yes, he certainly seems to be relaxing from the cares of State."

NARRATOR

But why, why does he have to relax with Loola? Vile brute and faithless strumpet! But there is at least one consolation—and to a shy man, plagued with desires he dares not act upon, a very great consolation: Loola's conduct is the proof of an accessibility which, in New Zealand, in academic circles, in the neighborhood of his Mother, could only be furtively dreamed about as something altogether too good to be true. And it is not only Loola who proves herself accessible. The same thing is being demonstrated, no less actively, no less vocally, by those mulatto girls, by Flossie, the plump and honey-colored Teuton, by that enormous Armenian matron, by the little tow-headed adolescent with the big blue eyes. . . .

"Yes, that's our Chief," says the Arch-Vicar bitterly. "Until he and the other pigs stop being possessed, the Church just takes over."

Incorrigibly cultured, in spite of his overwhelming desire to be out there with Loola—or almost anyone else, if it comes to that—Dr. Poole makes an apt remark about the Spiritual Authority and the Temporal Power.

The Arch-Vicar ignores it.

"Well," he says briskly, "it's time I got down to business."

He calls a Postulant, who hands him a tallow dip, then crosses over to the altar at the east end of the shrine. Upon it stands a single candle of yellow beeswax, three or four feet high and disproportionately thick. The Arch-Vicar genuflects, lights the candle, makes the sign of the horns, then comes back to where Dr. Poole is staring out, wide-eyed with fascinated horror and shocked concupiscence, at the spectacle in the arena.

"Stand aside, please."

Dr. Poole obeys.

A Postulant slides back first one door, then the other. The Arch-Vicar steps forward and stands in the center of the opening, touching the gilded horns of his tiara. From the musicians on the steps of the High Altar comes a shrill screeching of thighbone recorders. The noises of the crowd die away into a silence that is only occasionally punctuated by the bestial utterance of some joy or anguish too savagely violent to be repressed. Antiphonally, the priests begin to chant.

SEMICHORUS I

This is the time,

SEMICHORUS II

For Belial is merciless,

SEMICHORUS I

Time for Time' ending.

SEMICHORUS II

In the chaos of lust.

SEMICHORUS I

This is the time,

SEMICHORUS II

For Belial is in your blood,

SEMICHORUS I

Time for the birth in you

SEMICHORUS II

Of the Others, the Aliens,

SEMICHORUS I

Of Itch, of Tetter,

SEMICHORUS II

Of tumid Worm.

SEMICHORUS I

This is the time,

SEMICHORUS II

For Belial hates you,

SEMICHORUS I

Time for the Soul's death,

SEMICHORUS II

For the Person to perish,

SEMICHORUS I

Sentenced by craving,

SEMICHORUS II

And pleasure is the hangman;

SEMICHORUS I

Time for the Enemy's

SEMICHORUS II

Total triumph,

SEMICHORUS I

For the Baboon to be master,

SEMICHORUS II

That monsters may be begotten.

SEMICHORUS I

Not your will, but His,

SEMICHORUS II

That you may all be lost forever.

From the crowd rises a loud unanimous "Amen."

"His curse be on you," the Arch-Vicar intones in his high-pitched voice, then moves back to the end of the shrine and mounts the throne that stands next to the altar. From outside we hear a confused shouting that grows louder and louder, and suddenly the shrine is invaded by a throng of corybantic worshipers. They rush to the altar, they tear off one another's aprons and fling them in a mounting pile at the foot of the Arch-Vicar's throne. NO, NO, NO—and for each NO there is a triumphant shout of "Yes," followed by an unequivocal gesture toward the nearest person of the opposite sex. In the distance the priests are monotonously chanting, "Not your will, but His, that you may all be lost forever"—again and again.

Close shot of Dr. Poole, as he watches the proceedings from a corner of the oratory.

Cut back to the crowd, face after mindless, ecstatic face enters the field of view and passes out again. And there, suddenly, is Loola's face—the eyes shining, the lips parted, the dimples wildly alive. She turns her head, she catches sight of Dr. Poole.

"Alfie!" she cries.

Her tone and expression evoke an equally rapturous response.

"Loola!"

They rush together in a passionate embrace. Seconds pass. Vaselinelike, the strains of the Good Friday music from *Parsifal* make themselves heard on the sound track.

Then the faces come unstuck, the Camera pulls back.

"Quick, quick!"

Loola seizes his arm and drags him toward the altar.

"The apron," she says.

Dr. Poole looks down at the apron, then, blushing as red as the NO embroidered upon it, averts his eyes.

"It seems so . . . so indecorous," he says.

He stretches out his hand, withdraws it, then changes his mind yet again. Taking a corner of the apron between his thumb and forefinger, he gives it a couple of feebly ineffective tweaks.

"Harder," she cries, "Much harder!"

With an almost frantic violence—for it is not only the apron that he is tearing away, it is also his mother's influence and all his inhibitions, all the conventions in which he has been brought up—Dr. Poole does as he is told. The stitching yields more easily than he had anticipated and he almost falls over backward. Recovering his balance, he stands there, looking in sheepish embarrassment from the little diaper that represents the Seventh Commandment into Loola's laughing face and then down again at the crimson prohibition. Cut back and forth: NO, dimples, NO, dimples, NO. . . .

"Yes!" shouts Loola triumphantly. "Yes!"

Snatching the apron out of his hand, she throws it down at the foot of the throne. Then with a "Yes" and another "Yes," she rips the patches from her chest and, turning to the altar, makes her reverence to the Candle.

Medium close shot from the back of Loola genu-
flecting. All at once an elderly man with a gray beard
rushes excitedly into the shot, tears the twin NO's off
the seat of her homespun pants and starts to drag her
toward the door of the shrine.

Giving him a slap in the face and a vigorous push,
Loola breaks away and for the second time throws
herself into Dr. Poole's arms.

"Yes?" she whispers.

And emphatically he answers, "Yes!"

They kiss, smile rapturously at each other, then
move in the direction of the darkness beyond the
sliding doors. As they pass the throne, the Arch-Vicar
leans down and, smiling ironically, taps Dr. Poole on
the shoulder.

"What about my field glasses?" he says.

Dissolve to a night scene of ink-black shadows and
expanses of moonlight. In the background stands the
moldering pile of the Los Angeles County Museum.
Amorously interlaced, Loola and Dr. Poole enter the
shot, then pass into impenetrable darkness. Silhouettes
of men pursuing women, or women throwing themselves on men, appear for a moment and vanish. To
the accompaniment of the Good Friday music we hear
a rising and falling chorus of grunts and moans, of
explosively shouted obscenities and long-drawn howls
of agonizing delight.

NARRATOR

Consider the birds. What a delicacy in their love-
making, what old-world chivalry! For although the
hormones produced within the body of the breeding
hen predispose her to sexual emotion, their effect is
neither so intense nor of so brief a duration as that
of the ovarian hormones in the blood of female mam-

mals during oestrus. Moreover, for obvious reasons, the cock bird is in no position to enforce his desires upon an unwilling hen. Hence the prevalence among male birds of bright plumage and of an instinct for courtship. And hence the conspicuous absence of these charming things among male mammals. For where, as in the mammals, the female's amorous desires and her attractiveness to the male sex are wholly determined by chemical means, what need is there of masculine beauty of the niceties of preliminary courtship?

Among humans every day of the year is potentially the mating season. Girls are not chemically predestined during a few days, to accept the advances of the first male who presents himself. Their bodies manufacture hormones in doses sufficiently small to leave even the most temperamental of them a certain freedom of choice. That is why, unlike his fellow mammals, man has always been a wooer. But now the gamma rays have changed all that. The hereditary patterns of man's physical and mental behavior have been given another form. Thanks to the supreme Triumph of Modern Science, sex has become seasonal, romance has been swallowed up by the oestrus and the female's chemical compulsion to mate has abolished courtship, chivalry, tenderness, love itself. *i. a female* —

At this moment a radiant Loola and a considerably disheveled Dr. Poole emerge from the shadows. A burly male, temporarily unattached, comes striding into the shot. At the sight of Loola, he stops. His mouth falls open, his eyes widen, he breathes heavily.

Dr. Poole gives the stranger one look, then turns nervously to his companion.

"I think perhaps it might be a good thing if we walked this way . . ."

Without a word the stranger rushes at him, gives him a push that sends him flying and takes Loola in his arms. She resists for a moment; then the chemicals in her blood impose their Categorical Imperative, and she ceases to struggle.

Making a noise like a tiger at feeding time, the stranger lifts her off her feet and carries her into the shadows.

Dr. Poole, who has had time to pick himself up, makes as though to follow, to wreak vengeance, to rescue the distressed victim. Then a combination of apprehension and modesty causes him to slacken his pace. If he advances, heaven knows what he may find himself intruding upon. And then that man, that hairy hulk of bone and muscle. . . . On the whole it might perhaps be wiser. . . . He comes to a halt and stands hesitant, not knowing what to do. Suddenly two beautiful young mulatto girls come running out of the County Museum and simultaneously throw their brown arms round his neck and cover his face with kisses.

"You great big beautiful bastard," they whisper in husky unison.

For a moment Dr. Poole hesitates between the inhibitory recollection of his mother, the fidelity to Loola prescribed by all the poets and novelists, and the warm, elastic Facts of Life. After about four seconds of moral conflict, he chooses, as we might expect, the Facts of Life. He smiles, he returns the kisses, he murmurs words which it would startle Miss Hook and almost kill his mother to hear, he encircles either body with an arm, caresses either bosom with hands that have never done anything of the kind except in unavowable imaginings. The noises of mating swell to a brief climax, then diminish. For a little while there is complete silence.

Accompanied by a train of Archimandrites, Familiars, Presbyters and Postulants, the Arch-Vicar and the Patriarch of Pasadena come pacing majestically into the shot. At the sight of Dr. Poole and the mulattos, they come to a halt. Making a grimace of disgusted abhorrence, the Patriarch spits on the ground. More tolerant, the Arch-Vicar only smiles ironically.

"Dr. Poole!" he flutes in his odd falsetto.

Guiltily, as though he had heard his mother calling, Dr. Poole drops those busy hands of his and, turning toward the Arch-Vicar, tries to assume an expression of airy innocence. "These girls," his smile is meant to imply, "who *are* these girls? Why, I don't even know their names. We were just having a little chat about the higher cryptogams, that's all."

"You great big beautiful . . ." begins a husky voice.

Dr. Poole coughs loudly and fends off the embrace that accompanies the words.

"Don't mind us," says the Arch-Vicar pleasantly. "After all, Belial Day comes but once a year."

Approaching, he touches the gilded horns of his tiara, then lays his hands on Dr. Poole's head.

"Yours," he says with a suddenly professional unctuousness, "has been an almost miraculously sudden conversion. Yes, almost miraculously." Then, changing his tone, "By the way," he adds, "we've had a bit of trouble with your friends from New Zealand. This afternoon somebody spotted a group of them in Beverly Hills. I guess they were looking for you."

"Yes, I suppose so."

"But they're not going to find you," says the Arch-Vicar genially. "One of our Inquisitors went out with a posse of Familiars to deal with them."

"What happened?" Dr. Poole anxiously inquires.

"Our men laid an ambush, let fly with arrows. One was killed, and the others made off with the wounded. I don't think we shall be bothered again. But just to make certain . . ." He beckons to two of his attendants. "Listen," he says. "There isn't going to be a rescue and there isn't going to be an escape. I make you responsible, do you understand?"

The two Postulants bow their heads.

"And now," says the Arch-Vicar, turning back to Dr. Poole, "we'll leave you to beget all the little monsters you can."

He winks, pats Dr. Poole on the cheek, then takes the Patriarch's arm and, followed by his retinue, moves away.

Dr. Poole stares after the retreating figures, then glances uneasily at the two Postulants who have been appointed to guard him.

Brown arms are thrown around his neck.

"You great big beautiful . . ."

"No, really. Not in public. Not with those men around!"

"What difference does that make?"

And before he has time to answer, husky, musky, dusky, the Facts of Life close in on him again, and in a complicated embrace, like some half reluctant, half blissfully consenting Laocoon, he is ravished away into the shadows. With an expression of disgust, the two Postulants simultaneously spit.

NARRATOR

L'ombre était nuptiale, auguste et solennelle

He is interrupted by a burst of frenzied caterwauling.

NARRATOR

When I look into the fishponds in my garden,
(And not mine only, for every garden is riddled
With eel holes and reflected moons), *methinks*
I see a Thing armed with a rake that seems,
Out of the ooze, out of the immanence
Among the eels of heaven, *to strike at me—*
At Me the holy, Me divine! And yet
How tedious is a guilty conscience! How
Tedious, for that matter, an unguilty one!
What wonder if the horror of the fishponds
Draws us toward the rake? And the Thing strikes,
And I, the uneasy Person, in the mud,
Or in the liquid moonlight, thankfully
Find others than myself to have that blind
Or radiant being.

Dissolve to a medium shot of Dr. Poole asleep on
the drifted sand at the foot of a towering wall of concrete. Twenty feet away one of his guards is also
sleeping. The other is absorbed in an ancient copy
of *Forever Amber.* The sun is already high in the
heavens and a close shot reveals a small green lizard
crawling over one of Dr. Poole's outstretched hands.
He does not stir, but lies as though dead.

NARRATOR

And this, too, is the beatific being of somebody
who most certainly isn't Alfred Poole D.Sc. For sleep
is one of the preconditions of the Incarnation, the
primary instrument of divine immanence. Sleeping, we
cease to live that we may be lived (how blessedly!)
by some nameless Other who takes this opportunity

to restore the mind to sanity and bring healing to the abused and self-tormented body.

From breakfast to bedtime you may be doing everything in your power to outrage Nature and deny the fact of your Glassy Essence. But even the angriest ape at last grows weary of his tricks and has to sleep. And, while he sleeps, the indwelling Compassion preserves him, willy nilly, from the suicide which, in his waking hours, he has tried so frantically hard to commit. Then the sun rises again, and our ape wakes up once more to his own self and the freedom of his personal will—to yet another day of trick playing or, if he chooses, to the beginnings of self-knowledge, to the first steps toward his liberation.

A peal of excited feminine laughter cuts short the Narrator's speech. The sleeper stirs and, at a second, louder outburst, starts into full wakefulness and sits up, looking around him in bewilderment, not knowing where he is. Again that laughter. He turns his head in the direction of the sound. In a long shot from his viewpoint we see his two brown-skinned friends of the previous night emerging at full speed from behind a sand dune and darting into the ruins of the County Museum. At their heels, in concentrated silence, runs the Chief. All three disappear from view.

The sleeping Postulant wakes up and turns to his companion.

"What's that?" he asks.

"The usual thing," the other answers, without looking up from *Forever Amber*.

As he speaks, shrill squeals reverberate through the cavernous halls of the Museum. The Postulants look at one another in silence, then simultaneously spit.

Cut back to Dr. Poole.

"My God," he says aloud, "my God!"
He covers his face with his hands.

NARRATOR

Into the satiety of this morning-after let loose a
rodent conscience and the principles learned at a
mother's knee—or not infrequently across it (head
downward and with shirt tails well tucked up), in
condign spankings, sadly and prayerfully administered,
but remembered, ironically enough, as the pretext and
accompaniment of innumerable erotic daydreams, each
duly followed by its remorse, and each remorse bring-
ing with it the idea of punishment and all its attendant
sensualities. And so on, indefinitely. Well, as I say,
let those loose into this, and the result may easily be
a religious conversion. But a conversion to what? Most
ignorant of what he is most assured, our poor friend
doesn't know. And here comes almost the last person
he would expect to help him to discover.

As the Narrator speaks this last sentence, Loola
enters the shot.
"Alfie!" she cries happily. "I was looking for you."
Cut briefly to the two Postulants, who look at her
for a moment with all the distaste of enforced con-
tinence, then turn away and expectorate.
Meanwhile, after one brief glance at those "linea-
ments of satisfied desire," Dr. Poole guiltily averts his
eyes.
"Good morning," he says in a tone of formal polite-
ness. "I hope you . . . you slept well?"
Loola sits down beside him, opens the leather bag
which she carries slung over her shoulder and extracts half a loaf of bread and five or six large oranges.
"Nobody can think of doing much cooking these

days," she explains. "It's just one long picnic until the cold season begins again."

"Quite, quite," says Dr. Poole.

"You must be awfully hungry," she goes on. "After last night."

Her dimples come out of hiding, as she smiles at him.

Hot and blushing with embarrassment, Dr. Poole hastily tries to change the subject of conversation.

"Those are beautiful oranges," he remarks. "In New Zealand they don't do really well except in the extreme . . ."

"There!" says Loola, interrupting him.

She hands him a thick hunk of bread, breaks off another for herself and bites into it with strong white teeth.

"It's good," she says with her mouth full. "Why don't you eat?"

Dr. Poole who realizes that, in effect, he is ravenously hungry, but who is unwilling, for the sake of decorum, to admit the fact too openly, nibbles daintily at his crust.

Loola snuggles against him and leans her head on his shoulder.

"It was fun, Alfie, wasn't it?" She takes another bite of bread and without waiting for him to answer, continues: "More fun with you than with any of the others. Did you think that too?"

She looks up at him tenderly.

Close shot from her viewpoint of Dr. Poole's expression of agonizing moral discomfort.

"Alfie!" she cries, "what's the matter?"

"Perhaps it would be better," he manages at last to say, "if we talked about something else."

118

Loola straightens herself up and looks at him for a few seconds intently and in silence.

"You think too much," she says at last. "You mustn't think. If you think, it stops being fun." The light suddenly goes out of her face. "If you think," she goes on in a low voice, "it's terrible, terrible. It's a terrible thing to fall into the hands of the living Evil. When I remember what they did to Polly and her baby . . ."

She shudders, her eyes fill with tears and she turns away.

NARRATOR

Those tears again, those symptoms of personality —the sight of them evokes a sympathy that is stronger than the sense of guilt.

Forgetting the Postulants, Dr. Poole draws Loola toward him and with whispered words, with the caresses one uses to quiet a crying child, tries to comfort her. He is so successful that, in a minute or two, she is lying quite still in the crook of his arm. Sighing happily, she opens her eyes, looks up at him and smiles with an expression of tenderness, to which the dimples add a ravishingly incongruous hint of mischief.

"This is what I've always dreamed of."

"It is?"

"But it never happened—it never *could* happen. Not till *you* came . . ." She strokes his cheek. "I wish your beard didn't have to grow," she adds. "You'll look like the other fellows then. But you aren't like them, you're quite different."

"Not so different as all that," says Dr. Poole.

He bends down and kisses her on the eyelids, on the throat, on the mouth—then draws back and looks down at her with an expression of triumphant masculinity.

"Not different in *that* way," she qualifies. "But different in *this* way." She pats his cheek again. "You and I sitting together and talking and being happy because you're you and I'm me. It doesn't happen here. Except . . . except . . ." She breaks off. Her face darkens. "Do you know what happens to people who are Hots?" she whispers.

This time it is Dr. Poole's turn to protest against thinking too much. He backs up his words with action.

Close shot of the embrace. Then cut to the two Postulants, staring disgustedly at the spectacle. As they spit, another Postulant enters the shot.

"Orders from His Eminence," he says, making the sign of the horns. "This assignment's over. You're to report back to headquarters."

Dissolve to the *Canterbury*. A wounded seaman, with an arrow still sticking in his shoulder, is being hoisted in a sling from the whaleboat to the deck of the schooner. On the deck lie two other victims of the Californians' archery—Dr. Cudworth with a wound in his left leg and Miss Hook. The latter has an arrow imbedded deeply in her right side. The doctor, as he bends over her, looks grave.

"Morphine," he says to his orderly. "Then we'll get her down to the surgery as quickly as we can . . ."

Meanwhile there has been a shouting of orders and suddenly we hear the noise of the donkey engine and the clanking of the anchor chain as it is wound round the capstan.

Ethel Hook opens her eyes and looks around her. An expression of distress appears on her pale face.

"You're not going to sail away and leave him?" she says. "But you can't, you can't!" She makes an effort to raise herself from the stretcher; but the movement causes so much pain that she falls back again, with a groan.

"Quiet, quiet," says the doctor soothingly, as he swabs her arm with alcohol.

"But he may still be alive," she feebly protests. "They can't desert him; they can't just wash their hands of him."

"Hold still," says the doctor and, taking the syringe from his orderly, he drives the needle into the flesh.

The clanking of the anchor chain rises to a crescendo as we dissolve to Loola and Dr. Poole.

"I'm hungry," says Loola, sitting up.

Reaching for her knapsack, she takes out what is left of the bread, breaks it in two, hands the larger fragment to Dr. Poole and sinks her teeth into the other. She finishes her mouthful and is about to start on another, when she changes her mind. Turning to her companion, she takes his hand and kisses it.

"What's that for?" he asks.

Loola shrugs her shoulders.

"I don't know. I just suddenly felt like that." She eats some more bread, then, after a ruminative silence, turns to him with the air of one who has just made an important and unexpected discovery.

"Alfie," she announces, "I believe I shall never want to say Yes to anyone except you."

Greatly moved, Dr. Poole leans forward, takes her hand and presses it to his heart.

"I feel I've only just discovered what life's all about," he says.

"Me too."

She leans against him, and like a miser irresistibly drawn to count his treasure yet once more, Dr. Poole runs his fingers through her hair, separating lock

from thick lock, lifting a curl and letting it fall back
noiselessly into its place.

NARRATOR

And so, by the dialectic of sentiment, these two
have rediscovered for themselves that synthesis of the
chemical and the personal, to which we give the names
of monogamy and romantic love. In her case it was
the hormone that excluded the person; in his, the person that could not come to terms with the hormone.
But now there is the beginning of a larger wholeness.

Dr. Poole reaches into his pocket and pulls out the
little volume which he rescued yesterday from the
furnace. He opens it, turns the pages and begins to
read aloud.

" 'Warm fragrance seems to fall from her light dress
And her loose hair; and where some heavy tress
The air of her own speed has disentwined,
The sweetness seems to satiate the faint wind;
And in the soul a wild odor is felt
Beyond the sense, like fiery dews that melt
Into the bosom of a frozen bud.' "

"What's that?" Loola asks.

"You!" He bends down and kisses her hair. " 'And
in the soul,' " he whispers, " 'a wild odor is felt beyond
the sense.' In the soul," he repeats.

"What's the soul?" Loola asks.

"Well . . ." He hesitates; then, deciding to let
Shelley give the answer, he resumes his reading.

" 'See where she stands, a mortal shape indued
With love and life and light and deity,
And motion which may change, but never die,

An image of some bright Eternity,
A shadow of some golden dream; a Splendor
Leaving the third sphere pilotless; a tender
Reflection of the eternal Moon of Love . . .'"

"But I don't understand a word of it," Loola complains.

"And until today," says Dr. Poole, smiling down at her, "until today, neither did I."

We dissolve to the exterior of the Unholy of Unholies, two weeks later. Several hundreds of bearded men and slatternly women are queued up, in double file, awaiting their turn to enter the shrine. The Camera passes down the long line of dull and dirty faces, then holds on Loola and Dr. Poole, who are in the act of passing through the sliding doors.

Within all is gloom and silence. Two by two the nymphs and prancing satyrs of a few short days ago shuffle despondently past an altar, whose mighty candle is now eclipsed by a tin extinguisher. At the foot of the Arch-Vicar's empty throne lies the heap of discarded Seventh Commandments. As the procession slowly passes, the Archimandrite in charge of Public Morals hands out to every male an apron and to every female an apron and four round patches.

"Out through the side door," he repeats to each recipient.

And out through the side door, when their turn comes, Loola and Dr. Poole duly go. There, in the sunshine, a score of Postulants are busily at work, with thread and needle, stitching aprons to waistbands, patches to trouser seats and shirt fronts.

The Camera holds on Loola. Three young seminarists in Toggenberg cassocks accost her as she emerges into the open air.

She hands her apron to the first, a patch to each

of the others. All three set to work simultaneously and with extraordinary rapidity. NO, NO and NO.

"Turn around, please."

Handing over her last patches, she obeys; and, while the apron specialist moves away to attend to Dr. Poole, the others ply their needles so diligently that, in half a minute, she is no less forbidding from behind than when seen from in front.

"There!"

"And there!"

The two clerical tailors step aside and reveal a close shot of their handiwork. NO NO. Cut back to the Postulants, who express their sentiments by spitting in unison, then turn toward the door of the shrine.

"Next lady, please."

Wearing a look of extreme dejection, the two inseparable mulatto girls step forward together.

Cut to Dr. Poole. Aproned and bearded with a fortnight's growth of hair, he walks over to where Loola is waiting for him.

"This way, please," says a shrill voice.

In silence they take their places at the end of yet another queue. Resignedly, two or three hundred persons are waiting to be assigned their tasks by the Grand Inquisitor's Chief Assistant in charge of Public Works. Three-horned and robed impressively in a white Saanen soutane, the great man is sitting with a couple of two-horned Familiars at a large table, on which stand several steel filing cabinets salvaged from the offices of the Providential Life Insurance Company.

A series of montage shots exhibits, in twenty seconds, the slow, hour-long advance of Loola and Dr. Poole towards the well-spring of Authority. And now at last they have reached their destination. Close shot of the

Grand Inquisitor's Special Assistant as he tells Dr.
Poole to report to the Director of Food Production
at his office in the ruins of the Administration Building
of the University of Southern California. This gentleman will see that the botanist gets a laboratory, a
plot of ground for his experimental planting, and up
to four laborers to perform the manual work.

"Up to four laborers," the prelate repeats, "Though
at ordinary times . . ."

Unauthorized, Loola breaks into the conversation.

"Oh, let me be one of the laborers," she begs.
"Please."

The Grand Inquisitor's Special Assistant gives her
a long withering look, then turns to his Familiars.

"And who, pray, is this young vessel of the Unholy
Spirit?" he asks.

One of the Familiars extracts Loola's card from
the file and provides the relevant information. Aged
eighteen and hitherto sterile, the vessel in question
is reported to have associated during one off-season
with a notorious Hot, who was later liquidated while
trying to resist arrest. Nothing however was ever
proved against the said vessel and its conduct has
been generally satisfactory. Said vessel has been employed, for the past year, as a miner of cemeteries
and is to be similarly employed during the coming
season.

"But I want to work with Alfie," she protests.

"You seem to forget," says the first Familiar, "that
this is a Democracy . . ."

"A Democracy," adds his colleague, "in which every
proletarian enjoys perfect freedom."

"True freedom."

"Freely doing the will of the Proletariat."

"And *vox proletariatus, vox Diaboli.*"

"While, of course, *vox Diaboli, vox Ecclesiae.*"

"And we here are the Church's representatives."

"So you see."

"But I'm tired of cemeteries," the girl insists. "I'd like to dig up live things for a change."

There is a brief silence. Then the Grand Inquisitor's Special Assistant bends down and, from under his chair, produces a very large consecrated bull's pizzle, which he lays on the table before him. Then he turns to his subordinates.

"Correct me if I'm wrong," he says. "But my impression is that any vessel rejecting proletarian liberty is liable to twenty-five lashes for each and every such offence."

There is another silence. Pale and wide-eyed, Loola stares at the instrument of torture, then looks away, makes an effort to speak, finds herself voiceless and, swallowing hard, tries again.

"I won't resist," she manages to bring out. "I really *want* to be free."

"Free to go on mining cemeteries?"

She nods affirmatively.

"There's a good vessel!" says the Special Assistant.

Loola turns to Dr. Poole and, for a few seconds, they look into one another's eyes without speaking.

"Good-by, Alfie," she whispers at last.

"Good-by, Loola."

Two more seconds pass; then she drops her eyes and walks away.

"And now," says the Special Assistant to Dr. Poole, "we can get back to business. At ordinary times, as I was saying, you would be expected to make use of not more than two laborers. Do I make myself clear?"

Dr. Poole inclines his head.

We dissolve to a laboratory in which the sophomores of the University of Southern California once pursued the study of Elementary Biology. There are the usual sinks and tables, Bunsen burners and balances, cages for mice and guinea pigs, glass tanks for tadpoles. But the dust is thick over everything and scattered about the room lie half a dozen skeletons, still associated with the crumbling remains of slacks and sweaters, of Nylons and costume jewelry and brassieres.

The door opens and Dr. Poole enters, followed by the Director of Food Production, an elderly, grey-bearded man wearing homespun trousers, the standard apron and a cutaway coat that must once have belonged to the English butler of some twentieth-century motion picture executive.

"A little messy, I'm afraid," says the Director apologetically. "But I'll have the bones cleared out this afternoon and to-morrow the charvessels can dust off the tables and wash the floors."

"Quite," says Dr. Poole, "quite."

Dissolve to the same room a week later. The skeletons have been removed and thanks to the charvessels the floors, walls and furniture are almost clean. Dr. Poole has three distinguished visitors. Wearing his four horns and the brown, Anglo-Nubian habit of the Society of Moloch, the Arch-Vicar is seated beside the Chief, who is dressed in the much bemedalled uniform of a Rear-Admiral of the United States Navy, recently disinterred from Forest Lawn. At a respectful distance behind and to one side of the two Heads of Church and State sits the Director of Food Production, still disguised as a butler. Facing them, in the posture of a French Academician preparing to read his latest production to some choice and privileged audience, sits Dr. Poole.

"Shall I begin?" he asks.

The heads of Church and State exchange glances; then turn to Dr. Poole and simultaneously nod their assent. He opens his notebook and adjusts his spectacles.

"Notes on Soil Erosion and Plant Pathology in Southern California," he reads aloud. "Followed by a Preliminary Report on the Agricultural Situation and a Plan of Remedial Action for the Future. By Alfred Poole D.Sc. Assistant Professor of Botany at the University of Auckland."

As he reads, we dissolve to a slope among the foothills of the San Gabriel Mountains. Naked but for a cactus here and there, the stony ground lies dead and mangled in the sunshine. A network of ramifying gullies furrows the hillside. Some of them are still in the infancy of erosion, others have cut their way deep into the ground. The ruins of a substantial house, half of which has already been engulfed, stand precariously at the edge of one of these strangely fretted canyons. In the plain, at the foot of the hill, dead walnut trees emerge from the dried mud in which successive rains have buried them.

Over the shot we hear the sonorous drone of Dr. Poole's voice.

"In true symbiosis," he is saying, "there is a mutually beneficial relationship between two associated organisms. The distinguishing mark of parasitism, on the other hand, is that one organism lives at the expense of another. In the end this one-sided relationship proves fatal to both parties; for the death of the host cannot but result in the death of the parasite by which it has been killed. The relationship between modern man and the planet, of which, until so recently, he regarded himself as the master, has been that, not of symbiotic partners, but of tapeworm and infested dog, of fungus and blighted potato."

Cut back to the Chief. Within its nest of curly black beard, the red-lipped mouth has opened into an enormous yawn. Over the shot Dr. Poole reads on.

"Ignoring the obvious fact that his devastation of natural resources would, in the long run, result in the ruin of his civilization and even in the extinction of his species, modern man continued, generation after generation, to exploit the earth in such a way that . . ."

"Couldn't you make it a bit snappier?" asks the Chief.

Dr. Poole begins by looking offended. Then he remembers that he is a condemned captive on probation among savages, and forces a nervous smile.

"Perhaps it might be best," he says, "if we passed without more ado to the section on Plant Pathology."

"I don't care," says the Chief, "so long as you make it snappy."

"Impatience," pipes the Arch-Vicar sententiously, "is one of Belial's favorite vices."

Dr. Poole, meanwhile, has turned over three or four pages and is ready to start again.

"Given the existing state of the soil, yield per acre would be abnormally low, even if the principal food plants were completely healthy. But they are not healthy. After viewing crops in the field, after inspecting grains, fruits and tubers in storage, after examining botanical specimens under an almost undamaged pre-Thing microscope, I feel certain that there is only one explanation for the number and variety of plant diseases now rampant in the area—namely, deliberate infection of the crops by means of fungus bombs, bacteria-bearing aerosols and the release of many species of virus-carrying aphides and other insects. Otherwise how account for the prevalence and extreme virulence of *Giberella Saubinettii* and *Puccinia graminis?* Of *Phytophthora infestans* and *Synchitrium endobioticum?* Of all the mosaic diseases due to viruses? Of *Bacillus amylovorus, Bacillus carotovorus, Pseudomonas citri, Pseudomonas tumefaciens, Bacterium . . ."*

Cutting short his recitation almost before it has begun, the Arch-Vicar interrupts him.

"And you still maintain," he says, "that these people weren't possessed by Belial!" He shakes his head. "It's incredible how prejudice can blind even the most intelligent, the most highly educated . . ."

"Yes, yes, we know all that," says the Chief impatiently. "But now let's cut all the cackle and get down to practical business. What can you do about all this?"

Dr. Poole clears his throat.

"The task," he says impressively, "will be long-drawn and extremely arduous."

"But I want more food *now*," says the Chief imperiously. "I've got to have it this very year."

Somewhat apprehensively Dr. Poole is forced to tell him that disease-resisting varieties of plants cannot be bred and tested in under ten or twelve years. And meanwhile there is the question of the land; the erosion is destroying the land, erosion must be checked at all costs. But the labor of terracing and draining and composting is enormous and must go on unremittingly, year after year. Even in the old days, when manpower and machinery were plentiful, people had failed to do what was necessary to preserve the fertility of the soil.

"It wasn't because they couldn't," puts in the Arch-Vicar. "It was because they didn't want to. Between World War II and World War III they had all the time and all the equipment they needed. But they preferred to amuse themselves with power politics, and what were the consequences?" He counts off the answers on his thick fingers. "Worse malnutrition for more people. More political unrest. Resulting in more aggressive nationalism and imperialism. And finally the Thing. And why did they choose to destroy themselves? Because that was what Belial wanted them to do, because He had taken possession . . ."

The Chief holds up his hand.

"Please, please," he protests. "This isn't a course in Apologetics or Natural Diabology. We're trying to *do* something."

"And unfortunately the doing will take a long time," says Dr. Poole.

"How long?"

"Well, in five years you might find yourself holding your own against erosion. In ten years there'd be a perceptible improvement. In twenty years, some of your land might be back to as much as seventy per cent of its original fertility. In fifty years . . ."

"In fifty years," puts in the Arch-Vicar, "the deformity rate will be double what it is at present. And in a hundred years the triumph of Belial will be complete. But complete!" he repeats with a childlike giggle. He makes the sign of the horns and gets up from his chair. "But meanwhile I'm all for this gentleman doing everything he can."

Dissolve to the Hollywood Cemetery. Trucking shot of the monuments, with which our earlier visit to the graveyard has already made us familiar.

Medium close shot of the statue of Hedda Boddy. The Camera drops from the figure to the pedestal and the inscription.

". . . . affectionately known as Public Sweetheart Number One. 'Hitch your wagon to a Star.' "

Over the shot we hear the sound of a spade being thrust into the ground, then the rattle of sand and gravel as the earth is tossed aside.

The Camera pulls back, and we see Loola standing in a three-foot hole, wearily digging.

The sound of footsteps makes her look up. Flossie, the plump girl of the earlier sequence, enters the shot.

"Getting on all right?" she asks.

Loola nods without speaking and wipes her forehead with the back of her hand.

"When you hit the pay dirt," the plump girl goes on, "come and report to us."

"It'll take at least an hour more," says Loola gloomily.

"Well, keep at it, kid," says Flossie in the maddeningly hearty tones of a person delivering a pep talk. "Put your back into it. Prove to them that a vessel can do as much as a man! If you work well," she goes on encouragingly, "maybe the Superintendent will let you keep the Nylons. Look at the pair *I* got this morning!"

She pulls the coveted trophies from her pocket. Except for a greenish discoloration around the toes, the stockings are in perfect condition.

"Oh!" cries Loola in envious admiration.

"But we didn't have any luck with the jewelry," says Flossie, as she puts the stockings away again. "Just the wedding ring and a rotten little bracelet. Let's hope this one won't let us down."

She pats the Parian stomach of Public Sweetheart Number One.

"Well, I must get back," she continues. "We're digging for the vessel who's buried under that red stone cross—you know, the big one, near the north gate."

Loola nods.

"I'll be there as soon as I make a strike," she says.

Whistling the tune of "When I survey the Wondrous Horns," the plump girl walks out of the shot. Loola sighs, and resumes her digging.

Very softly, a voice pronounces her name.

She starts violently and turns in the direction from which the sound has come.

Medium shot from her viewpoint of Dr. Poole advancing cautiously from behind the tomb of Rudolf Valentino.

Cut back to Loola.

She flushes, then turns deathly pale. Her hand goes to her heart.

"Alfie," she whispers.

He enters the shot, jumps into the grave beside her and, without a word, takes her in his arms. The kiss is passionate. Then she hides her face against his shoulder.

"I thought I should never see you any more," she says in a breaking voice.

"What did you take me for?"

He kisses her again, then holds her at arm's length and looks into her face.

"Why are you crying?" he asks.

"I can't help it."

"You're lovelier even than I remembered."

She shakes her head, unable to speak.

"Smile," he commands.

"I can't."

"Smile, smile. I want to see them again."

"See what?"

"Smile!"

With an effort, but full of a passionate tenderness, Loola smiles up at him.

In her cheeks the dimples emerge from the long hibernation of her sorrow.

"There they are," he cries in delight, "there they are!"

Delicately, like a blind man reading Herrick in Braille, he passes a finger across her cheek. Loola smiles more effortlessly, the dimple deepens under his touch. He laughs with pleasure.

At the same moment the whistled tune of "When I behold the Wondrous Horns" swells from a distant *pianissimo* through *piano* to *mezzo forte*.

An expression of terror appears on Loola's face.

"Quick, quick!" she whispers.

With astonishing agility Dr. Poole scrabbles out of the grave.

By the time the plump girl re-enter:s the shot he is leaning in a studiedly casual attitude against the monument to Public Sweetheart Number One. Below him, in the pit, Loola is digging like mad.

"I forgot to tell you that we're knocking off for lunch in half an hour," Flossie begins.

Then, catching sight of Dr. Poole, she utters an exclamation of surprise.

"Good morning," says Dr. Poole politely.

There is a silence. Flossie looks from Dr. Poole to Loola and from Loola back to Dr. Poole.

"What are *you* doing here?" she asks suspiciously.

"I'm on my way to St. Azazel's," he answers. "The

Arch-Vicar sent a message that he wanted me to attend his three lectures to the Seminarists. Belial in History—that's the subject of them."

"You've chosen a very funny way to get to St. Azazel's."

"I was looking for the Chief," Dr. Poole explains.

"Well, he's not here," says the plump girl.

There is another silence.

"In that case," says Dr. Poole, "I'd better be trotting along. Mustn't keep either of you young ladies from your duties," he adds with an artificial and entirely unconvincing brightness. "Good-by. Good-by."

He bows to the two girls, then, assuming an air of easy nonchalance, walks away.

Flossie looks after him in silence, then turns severely to Loola.

"Now listen, kid," she begins.

Loola stops digging and looks up from the grave.

"What is it, Flossie," she asks with an expression of uncomprehending innocence.

"What is it?" the other echoes derisively. "Tell me, what's written on your apron?"

Loola looks down at her apron, then back at Flossie. Her face reddens with embarrassment.

"What's written on it?" the plump girl insists.

" 'No!' "

"And what's written on those patches?"

" 'No!' " Loola repeats.

"And on the other ones, when you turn around?"

" 'No!' "

"No, no, no, no, no," says the plump girl emphatically. "And when the Law says no, it means no. You know that as well as I do, don't you."

Loola nods her head without speaking.

"Say you know it," the other insists. "Say it."

"Yes, I know it," Loola brings out at last in a barely audible voice.

"Good. Then don't pretend you haven't been warned. And if that foreign Hot ever comes prowling around you again, just let me know. *I'll* see to him."

We dissolve to the interior of St. Azazel's. Once the Church of Our Lady of Guadalupe, St. Azazel's has undergone only the most superficial of alterations. In the chapels, the plaster figures of St. Joseph, the Magdalen, St. Anthony of Padua and St. Rose of Lima have merely been painted red and fitted with horns. On the high altar nothing has been changed except that the crucifix has been replaced by a pair of enormous horns carved out of cedar wood and hung with a wealth of rings and wrist watches, of bracelets, chains, earrings and necklaces, mined from the cemeteries or found in association with old bones and the moldering remnants of jewel boxes.

In the body of the church some fifty Toggenberg-robed seminarists—with Dr. Poole, incongruously bearded and in tweeds, in the middle of the front row—are sitting with bowed heads while, from the pulpit, the Arch-Vicar pronounces the final words of his lecture.

"For as in the Order of Things all might, if they had so desired, have lived, so also in Belial all have been, or inevitably shall be, made to die. Amen."

There is a long silence. Then the Master of Novices rises. With a great rustling of fur, the seminarists follow suit and start to walk, two by two, and with the most perfect decorum, toward the west door.

Dr. Poole is about to follow them, when he hears a high childish voice calling his name.

Turning, he sees the Arch-Vicar beckoning from the steps of the pulpit.

"Well, what did you think of the lecture?" squeaks the great man, as Dr. Poole approaches.

"Very fine."

"Without flattery?"

"Really and truly."

The Arch-Vicar smiles with pleasure.

"I'm glad to hear it," he says.

"I specially liked what you said about religion in the nineteenth and twentieth centuries—the retreat from Jeremiah to the Book of Judges, from the personal and therefore the universal to the national and therefore the internecine."

The Arch-Vicar nods.

"Yes, it was a pretty close shave," he says. "If they'd stuck to the personal and the universal, they'd have been in harmony with the Order of Things, and the Lord of Flies would have been done for. But fortunately Belial had plenty of allies—the nations, the churches, the political parties. He used their prejudices. He exploited their ideologies. By the time they'd developed the atomic bomb, he had people back in the state of mind they were in before 900 B.C."

"And then," says Dr. Poole, "I liked what you said about the contacts between East and West—how He persuaded each side to take only the worst the other had to offer. So the East takes Western nationalism, Western armaments, Western movies and Western Marxism; the West takes Eastern despotism, Eastern superstitions and Eastern indifference to individual life. In a word, He saw to it that mankind should make the worst of both worlds."

"Just think if they'd made the best!" squeaks the Arch-Vicar. "Eastern mysticism making sure that West-

137

ern science should be properly used; the Eastern art of living refining Western energy; Western individualism tempering Eastern totalitarianism." He shakes his head in pious horror. "Why, it would have been the kingdom of heaven. Happily the grace of Belial was stronger than the Other One's grace."

He chuckles shrilly; then laying a hand on Dr. Poole's shoulder, he starts to walk with him toward the vestry.

"You know, Poole," he says, "I've got to be very fond of you." Dr. Poole mumbles his embarrassed acknowledgements.

"You're intelligent, you're well educated, you know all kinds of things that we've never learned. You could be very useful to me and, on my side, I could be very useful to you—that is," he adds, "if you were to become one of us."

"One of you?" Dr. Poole repeats doubtfully.

"Yes, one of *us.*"

Comprehension dawns on an expressive close-up of Dr. Poole's face. He utters a dismayed "Oh!"

"I won't disguise from you," says the Arch-Vicar, "that the surgery involved is not entirely painless, nor wholly without danger. But the advantages to be gained by entering the priesthood would be so great as to outweigh any trifling risk or discomfort. Nor must we forget . . ."

"But, Your Eminence . . ." Dr. Poole protests.

The Arch-Vicar holds up a plump, damp hand.

"One moment, please," he says severely.

His expression is so forbidding that Dr. Poole hastens to apologize.

"I beg your pardon."

"Granted, my dear Poole, granted."

Once again the Arch-Vicar is all amiability and condescension.

"Well, as I was saying," he goes on, "we must not forget that, if you were to undergo what I may call a physiological conversion, you would be delivered from all the temptations to which, as an unmutated male, you will most certainly be exposed."

"Quite, quite," Dr. Poole agrees. "But I can assure you . . ."

"Where temptations are concerned," says the Arch-Vicar sententiously, "nobody can assure anyone of anything."

Dr. Poole remembers his recent interview with Loola in the cemetery, and feels himself blushing.

"Isn't that rather a sweeping statement?" he says without too much conviction.

The Arch-Vicar shakes his head.

"In these matters," he says, "one can never be too sweeping. And let me remind you of what happens to those who succumb to such temptations. The bulls' pizzles and the burying squad are always in readiness. And that is why, in your own interests, for your future happiness and peace of mind, I advise you—nay, I beg and implore you—to join our Order."

There is a silence. Dr. Poole swallows hard.

"I should like to be able to think it over," he says at last.

"Of course, of course," the Arch-Vicar agrees. "Take your time. Take a week."

"A week? I don't think I could decide in a week."

"Take two weeks," says the Arch-Vicar, and when Dr. Poole still shakes his head, "Take four," he adds, "take six, if you like. I'm in no hurry. I'm only concerned about you." He pats Dr. Poole on the shoulder. "Yes, my dear fellow, about *you.*"

Dissolve to Dr. Poole at work in his experimental garden, planting out tomato seedlings. Nearly six weeks have passed. His brown beard is considerably more luxuriant, his tweed coat and flannel trousers considerably dirtier, than when we saw him last. He wears a gray homespun shirt and moccasins of local manufacture.

When the last of his seedlings is in the ground, he straightens himself up, stretches, rubs his aching back, then walks slowly to the end of the garden and stands there motionless, looking out at the view.

In a long shot, we see, as it were through his eyes, a wide prospect of deserted factories and crumbling houses, backed in the distance by a range of mountains that recedes, fold after fold, toward the east. The shadows are gulfs of indigo, and in the richly golden lights the far-off details stand out distinct and small and perfect, like the images of things in a convex mirror. In the foreground, delicately chased and stippled by the almost horizontal light, even the baldest patches of parched earth reveal an unsuspected sumptuousness of texture.

NARRATOR

There are times, and this is one of them, when the world seems purposefully beautiful, when it is as though some mind in things had suddenly chosen to make manifest, for all who choose to see, the supernatural reality that underlies all appearances.

Dr. Poole's lips move and we catch the low murmur of his words.

" 'For love and beauty and delight
There is no death nor change; their might

140

Exceeds our organs, which endure
No light, being themselves obscure.' "

He turns and walks back toward the entrance to
the garden. Before opening the gate, he looks cautiously around him. There is no sign of an unfriendly
observer. Reassured, he slips out and almost immediately turns into a winding path between sand
dunes. Once again his lips move.

" 'I am the Earth,
Thy mother; she within whose stony veins
To the last fiber of the loftiest tree,
Whose thin leaves trembled in the frozen air,
Joy ran, as blood within a living frame,
When thou didst from her bosom, like a cloud
Of glory, arise, a spirit of keen joy.' "

From the footpath Dr. Poole emerges into a street
flanked by small houses, each with its garage and
each surrounded by the barren space that was once
a plot of grass and flowers.

" 'A spirit of keen joy,' " he repeats and then sighs
and shakes his head.

NARRATOR

Joy? But joy was murdered long ago. All that sur-
vives is the laughter of demons about the whipping
posts, the howling of the possessed as they couple in
the darkness. Joy is only for those whose life accords
with the given Order of the world. For you there,
the clever ones who think you can improve upon that
Order, for you, the angry ones, the rebellious, the
disobedient, joy is fast becoming a stranger. Those
who are doomed to reap the consequences of your
fantastic tricks will never so much as suspect its

existence. Love, Joy and Peace—these are the fruits of the spirit that is your essence and the essence of the world. But the fruits of the ape-mind, the fruits of the monkey's presumption and revolt are hate and unceasing restlessness and a chronic misery tempered only by frenzies more horrible than itself.

Dr. Poole, meanwhile, continues on his way.

" 'The world is full of woodmen,' " he says to himself,
" 'The world is full of woodmen, who expel
Love's gentle dryads from the trees of life
And vex the nightingales in every dell.' "

NARRATOR

Woodmen with axes, dryad-killers with knives, nightingale-vexers with scalpels and surgical scissors.

Dr. Poole shudders and, like a man who feels himself dogged by some malevolent presence, quickens his pace. Suddenly he halts and once more looks about him.

NARRATOR

In a city of two and a half million skeletons the presence of a few thousands of the living is hardly perceptible. Nothing stirs. The silence is total and, in the midst of all these cozy little bourgeois ruins, seems conscious and in some sort conspiratorial.

His pulses quickened by hope and the fear of disappointment, Dr. Poole turns off the road and hurries along the drive that leads to the garage of Number 1993. Sagging on their rusted hinges, the double doors stand ajar. He slips between them into a musty twilight. Through a hole in the west wall of the garage a thin pencil of late afternoon sunshine reveals the left front wheel of a Super de Luxe Four-Door Chevrolet Sedan and, on the ground beside it, two skulls, one an adult's, the other evidently a child's. Dr. Poole opens the only one of the four doors which is not jammed and peers into the darkness within.

"Loola!"

He climbs into the car, sits down beside her on the disintegrated upholstery of the back seat, and takes her hand in both of his.

"Darling!"

She looks at him without speaking. In her eyes there is an expression almost of terror.

"So you were able to get away after all?"

"But Flossie still suspects something."

"Damn Flossie!" says Dr. Poole in a tone that is intended to be carefree and reassuring.

"She kept asking questions," Loola goes on. "I told her I was going out to forage for needles and cutlery."

"But all you've found is me."

He smiles at her tenderly and raises her hand to his lips; but Loola shakes her head.

"Alfie—please!"

Her tone is a supplication. He lowers her hand without kissing it.

"And yet you do love me, don't you?"

She looks at him with eyes that are wide with a frightened bewilderment, then turns away.

"I don't know, Alfie, I don't know."

"Well, *I* know," says Dr. Poole decidedly. "I know I love you. I know I want to be with you. Always. Till death do us part," he adds with all the fervor of an introverted sexualist suddenly converted to objectivity and monogamy.

143

Loola shakes her head again.

"All I know is that I oughtn't to be here."

"But that's nonsense!"

"No, it isn't. I oughtn't to be here now. I oughtn't to have come those other times. It's against the Law. It's against everything that people think. It's against Him," she adds after a moment's pause. An expression of agonized distress appears on her face. "But then why did He make me so that I could feel this way about you? Why did He make me like those— like those—" She cannot bring herself to utter the abhorred word. "I used to know one of them," she goes on in a low voice. "He was sweet—almost as sweet as you are. And then they killed him."

"What's the good of thinking about other people?" says Dr. Poole. "Let's think about ourselves. Let's think how happy we could be, how happy we actually were two months ago. Do you remember? The moonlight . . . And how dark it was in the shadows! And in the soul a wild odor is felt beyond the sense . . . !"

"But we weren't doing wrong then."

"We're not doing wrong now."

"No, no, it's quite different now."

"It isn't different," he insists. "I don't feel any different from what I did then. And neither do you."

"I do," she protests—too loudly to carry conviction.

"No, you don't."

"I do."

"You don't. You've just said it. You're not like these other people—thank God!"

"Alfie!"

She makes a propitiatory sign of the horns.

"They've been turned into animals," he goes on. "You haven't. You're still a human being—a normal human being with normal human feelings."

"I'm not."

"Yes, you are."

"It isn't true," she wails. "It isn't true."

She covers her face with her hands and starts to cry.

"He'll kill me," she sobs.

"Who'll kill you?"

Loola raises her head and looks apprehensively over her shoulder, through the rear window of the car.

"*He* will. He knows everything we do, everything we even think or feel."

"Maybe He does," says Dr. Poole, whose Liberal-Protestant views about the Devil have been considerably modified during the past few weeks. "But if we feel and think and do the right thing, He can't hurt us."

"But what *is* the right thing?" she asks.

For a second or two he smiles at her without speaking.

"Here and now," he says at last, "the right thing is *this*."

He slips an arm about her shoulders and draws her toward him.

"No, Alfie, no!"

Panic-stricken, she tries to free herself; but he holds her tight.

"This is the right thing," he repeats. "It mightn't always and everywhere be the right thing. But here and now it is—definitely."

He speaks with the force and authority of complete conviction. Never in all his uncertain and divided life has he thought so clearly or acted so decisively.

Loola suddenly ceases to struggle.

"Alfie, are you *sure* it's all right? Are you absolutely sure?"

"Absolutely sure," he replies from the depths of his new, self-validating experience. Very gently he strokes her hair.

"'A mortal shape,'" he whispers, "'indued with love and life and light and deity. A Metaphor of Spring and Youth and Morning, a Vision like incarnate April.'"

"Go on," she whispers.

Her eyelids are closed, her face wears that look of supernatural serenity which one sees upon the faces of the dead.

Dr. Poole begins again.

"'And we will talk, until thought's melody
Become too sweet for utterance, and it die
In words, to live again in looks, which dart
With thrilling tone into the voiceless heart,
Harmonizing silence without a sound.
Our breath shall intermix, our bosoms bound
And our veins beat together, and our lips
With other eloquence than words, eclipse
The soul that burns between them, and the wells
Which boil under our being's inmost cells,
The fountains of our deepest life, shall be
Confused in Passion's golden purity;
As mountain springs under the morning sun,
We shall become the same, we shall be one
Spirit within two frames, oh! Wherefore two?'"

There is a long silence. Suddenly Loola opens her eyes, looks at him intently for a few seconds, then throws her arms round his neck and kisses him passionately on the mouth. But even as he clasps her more closely, she breaks away from him and retreats to her end of the seat.

He tries to approach, but she holds him at arm's length.

"It can't be right," she says.

"But it *is* right."

She shakes her head.

"It's too good to be right, I should be too happy if it were. He doesn't want us to be happy." There is a pause. "Why do you say He can't hurt us?"

"Because there's something stronger than He is."

"Something stronger?" She shakes her head. "That was what He was always fighting against—and He won."

"Only because people helped Him to win. But they don't have to help Him. And, remember, He can never win for good."

"Why not?"

"Because He can never resist the temptation of carrying evil to the limit. And whenever evil is carried to the limit, it always destroys itself. After which the Order of Things comes to the surface again."

"But that's far away in the future."

"For the whole world, yes. But not for single individuals, not for you or me, for example. Whatever Belial may have done with the rest of the world, you and I can always work with the Order of Things not against it."

There is another silence.

"I don't think I understand what you mean," she says at last, "and I don't care." She moves back toward him and leans her head against his shoulder. "I don't care about anything," she goes on. "He can kill me if He wants to. It doesn't matter. Not now."

She raises her face towards his and, as he bends down to kiss her, the image on the screen fades into the darkness of a moonless night.

NARRATOR

L'ombre· était nuptiale, auguste et solennelle. But
this time it is a nuptial darkness whose solemnity is
marred by no caterwaulings, no *Liebestods,* no saxophones pleading for detumescence. The music with
which this night is charged is clear, but undescriptive;
precise and definite, but about realities that have no
name; all-embracingly liquid, but never viscous, without the slightest tendency to stick possessively to what
it touches and comprehends. A music with the spirit
of Mozart's, delicately gay among the constant im-
plications of tragedy; a music akin to Weber's, aristocratic and refined, and yet capable of the most
reckless joy and the completest realization of the
world's agony. And is there perhaps a hint of that
which, in the *Ave Verum Corpus,* in the *G-minor
Quintet,* lies beyond the world of *Don Giovanni?* Is
there a hint already of what (in Bach, sometimes, and
in Beethoven, in that final wholeness of art which is
analogous to holiness) transcends the Romantic inte-
gration of the tragic and the joyful, the human and
the daemonic? And when, in the darkness, the lover's
voice whispers again of

> a mortal form indued
> With love and life and light and deity,

is there already the beginning of an understanding
that beyond *Epipsychidion* there is *Adonais* and beyond *Adonais,* the wordless doctrine of the Pure in
Heart?

Dissolve to Dr. Poole's laboratory. Sunlight pours
through the tall windows, and is dazzlingly reflected
from the stainless steel barrel of the microscope on
the work table. The room is empty.

Suddenly the silence is broken by the sound of approaching footsteps; the door is opened and, still a butler on moccasins, the Director of Food Production looks in.

"Poole," he begins, "His Eminence has come to . . ."

He breaks off and an expression of astonishment appears on his face.

"He isn't here," he says to the Arch-Vicar who now follows him into the room.

The great man turns to the two Familiars in attendance on him.

"Go and see if Dr. Poole is in the experimental garden," he orders.

The Familiars bow, squeak, "Yes, Your Eminence," in unison, and go out.

The Arch-Vicar sits down and graciously motions to the Director to follow his example.

"I don't think I told you," he says; "I'm trying to persuade our friend here to enter religion."

"I hope Your Eminence doesn't mean to deprive us of his invaluable help in the field of food production," says the Director anxiously.

The Arch-Vicar reassures him.

"I'll see that he always has time to give you the advice you need. But meanwhile I want to make sure that the Church shall benefit by his talents and . . ."

The Familiars re-enter the room and bow.

"Well?"

"He isn't in the gardens, Your Eminence."

The Arch-Vicar frowns angrily at the Director, who quails under his look.

"I thought you said this was the day he worked in the laboratory?"

"It is, Your Eminence."

"Then why is he out?"

"I can't imagine, Your Eminence. I've never known him to change his schedule without telling me."

There is a silence.

"I don't like it," the Arch-Vicar says at last. "I don't like it at all." He turns to his Familiars. "Run back to Headquarters and have half a dozen men ride out on horseback to find him."

The Familiars bow, squeak simultaneously, and vanish.

"And as for you," says the Arch-Vicar, turning on the pale and abject figure of the Director, "if anything should have happened, you'll have to answer for it."

He rises in majestic wrath and stalks toward the door.

Dissolve to a series of montage shots.

Loola with her leather knapsack and Dr. Poole, with a pre-Thing army pack on his back, are climbing over a landslide that blocks one of those superbly engineered highways, whose remains still scar the flanks of the San Gabriel mountains.

We cut to a windswept crest. The two fugitives are looking down over the enormous expanse of the Mojave desert.

Next we find ourselves in a pine forest on the northern slope of the range. It is night. In a patch of moonlight between the trees, Dr. Poole and Loola lie sleeping under the same homespun blanket.

Cut to a rocky canyon, at the bottom of which flows a stream. The lovers have halted to drink and fill their water bottles.

And now we are in the foothills above the floor of the desert. Between the clumps of sage brush, the yuccas and the juniper bushes the walking is easy. Dr. Poole and Loola enter the shot, and the Camera

150

trucks with them as they come striding down the slope.

"Feet sore?" he asks solicitously.

"Not too bad."

She gives him a brave smile, and shakes her head. "I think we'd better stop pretty soon and eat something."

"Just as you think best, Alfie."

He pulls an antique map out of his pocket and studies it as he walks along.

"We're still a good thirty miles from Lancaster," he says. "Eight hours of walking. We've got to keep up our strength."

"And how far shall we get tomorrow?" Loola asks.

"A little beyond Mojave. And after that I reckon it'll take us at least two days to cross the Tehachapis and get to Bakersfield." He returns the map to his pocket. "I managed to get quite a lot of information out of the Director," he goes on. "He says those people up north are very friendly to runaways from Southern California. Won't give them back even when the government officially asks for them."

"Thank Bel . . . I mean, thank God," says Loola.

There is another silence. Suddenly Loola comes to a halt.

"Look! What's that?"

She points and from their viewpoint we see at the foot of a very tall Joshua tree, a slab of weathered concrete, standing crookedly at the head of an ancient grave, overgrown with bunch grass and buckwheat.

"Somebody must have been buried here," says Dr. Poole.

They approach and, in a close shot of the slab, we see, while Dr. Poole's voice reads aloud the following inscription:

WILLIAM TALLIS
1882-1948

Why linger, why turn back, why shrink, my Heart?
Thy hopes are gone before: from all things here
They have departed, thou shouldst now depart!

Cut back to the two lovers.

"He must have been a very sad man," says Loola.

"Perhaps not quite so sad as you imagine," says Dr. Poole, as he slips off his heavy pack and sits down beside the grave.

And while Loola opens her knapsack and takes out bread and fruit and eggs and strips of dried meat, he turns over the pages of his duodecimo Shelley.

"Here we are," he says at last. "It's the very next stanza after the one that's quoted here.

" 'That Light whose smile kindles the Universe
That Beauty in which all things work and move
That Benediction, which the eclipsing Curse
Of birth can quench not, that sustaining Love,
Which through the web of being blindly wove
By man and beast and earth and air and sea,
Burns bright or dim, as each are mirrors of
The fire for which all thirst, now beams on me
Consuming the last clouds of cold mortality.' "

There is a silence. Then Loola hands him a hard boiled egg. He cracks it on the headstone and, as he peels it, scatters the white fragments of the shell over the grave.